Praise for
Bestselling Author Carla Cassidy

"Solid storytelling and sympathetic, genuine
characters will draw readers in from the
start. . .this is one amazing read."
—*RT Book Reviews* on *A Real Cowboy*

"Carla Cassidy has made this an extremely hard
book to put down. The pages just flew past!
A very talented and colorful author!"
—*Fresh Fiction* on *Mercenary's Perfect Mission*

"Cassidy delivers with a one-two punch of
intriguing suspense and tantalizing romance.
A sure bet, this romantic read will have readers
rooting for a reunion."
—*RT Book Reviews* on *Scene of the Crime:
Baton Rouge*

"[An] action-packed romantic suspense starring
an amazing female and her deceiving beloved."
—*The Best Reviews* on *Deceived*

"[A] taut, fast-paced romantic thriller. . .romance
shines."
—*Publishers Weekly*

COWBOY AT ARMS

BY
CARLA CASSIDY

First Published in Great Britain 2016
By Mills & Boon, an imprint of HarperCollins*Publishers*
1 London Bridge Street, London, SE1 9GF

© 2016 Carla Bracale

ISBN: 978-0-263-91931-8

18-0316

Our policy is to use papers that are natural, renewable and recyclable products and made from wood grown in sustainable forests.The logging and manufacturing processes conform to the legal environmental regulations of the country of origin.

Printed and bound in Spain
by CPI, Barcelona

Carla Cassidy is a *New York Times* bestselling author who has written more than one hundred books for Mills & Boon. Carla believes the only thing better than curling up with a good book to read is sitting down at the computer with a good story to write. She's looking forward to writing many more books and bringing hours of pleasure to readers.

Chapter 1

Man up, Dusty Crawford commanded himself as he stared at the front door of the Bitterroot Café. It was almost nine o'clock on Friday night and the summer sun just barely skimmed the horizon in its downward descent.

As darkness slowly fell, the interior of the brightly lit café became more visible. He'd waited to arrive until late enough in the day that the dinner hour would be over and the popular eatery would be less crowded.

He'd wrestled stubborn cattle and faced more than one marauding cougar over the years, and yet the thought of the beautiful blonde waitress inside the café had him nearly shaking in his boots.

He turned his head at the sound of several doors

slamming nearby. He narrowed his gaze as he watched three cowboys amble from the parking lot toward the café's front door.

Zeke Osmond, Greg Albertson and Shep Harmon all worked on the ranch next to the Holiday spread where Dusty had worked and lived since he was fourteen years old. For the most part all of the men who were part of the Humes ranch were mean and liked nothing more than to stir up trouble wherever they went.

The Humes men were suspected of all kinds of mischief on the Holiday land, including tearing down fencing, setting nuisance fires and the occasional cattle disappearance.

As they went inside the building, Dusty shoved thoughts of them out of his head. He needed to focus on the reason he was here. After a little over six months of small talk whenever he ate at the café, tonight he was here to ask Trisha Cahill out on an official date.

He took off his black cowboy hat and set it on the passenger seat and then raked his hand through his hair. Drawing a deep breath for courage, he finally left his pickup truck and headed for the café door.

When he stepped inside, his nose was immediately assailed by the scents of fried potatoes and onions, a variety of simmering meats and a faint whiff of apples and cinnamon.

Even though it was late for dinner there was still a crowd at the tables and booths. This wasn't just a place to eat in the small town of Bitterroot, Oklahoma; it was also a place where folks came to visit with neighbors and catch up with the local gossip.

His gaze instantly found Trisha, who was taking an order from Steve Kaufman, a widower who lived alone and spent most evenings in the café sipping coffee and reading a book.

Dusty headed toward an empty booth that he knew was in Trisha's area and sat. He grabbed one of the plastic menus propped up between squeeze bottles of mustard and ketchup. He opened it even though he'd long ago memorized everything that the café had to offer.

Nerves jangled in the pit of his stomach. *You're being ridiculous*, he told himself. The worst thing that could happen was that Trisha would tell him in no uncertain terms that she had no interest in going out with him. He could live with that. He'd certainly survived much worse in his twenty-nine years on earth.

He closed the menu and returned it to its place and then looked up and smiled as Trisha approached his booth. "Hi, Dusty. You're a little later than usual tonight," she said. Her eyes were the color of a clear summer sky and filled with her casual friendliness.

"Yeah, I decided to skip Daisy's Friday night meatloaf dinner and I ate at the ranch instead," he replied. Her pale blond hair was pulled up into a slightly messy ponytail, and Dusty's fingers itched with the desire to release all of it from its confinement.

"So, what can I get for you?" she asked.

"I'll take one of Daisy's apple dumplings and a cup of coffee."

"I'll have it to you in just a jiffy." She turned and left his booth.

Dusty released a pent-up sigh. He'd ask her out after he'd eaten his dessert. Maybe by then a lot of the people would be gone and she'd be less busy.

Within minutes Dusty had his dumpling and coffee and Trisha had hurried to another table after serving him. As he ate he watched her taking care of her customers. She had a cheerful smile for everyone and she looked totally hot in her slim-fitting blue jeans and the red T-shirt with gold lettering advertising the café.

Despite the fact that he'd been interested in her for months, he really knew very little about her other than she lived in the Bitterroot Motel and had a young son and she was one of the most popular, well-liked waitresses at the café.

By the time he'd finished his dumpling and was nursing a second cup of coffee, the crowd had finally begun to thin out. He motioned to Trisha and she hurried over to his booth. "Ready for your check?" she asked.

"Actually, I was wondering if you had a minute to sit with me," he replied.

She looked around at the diners remaining in her area and then nodded. "Sure, I can take a few minutes."

It wasn't uncommon for her to occasionally sit and visit with Dusty when things were slow in the café. She slid into the opposite side of the booth and smiled at him once again. "It feels good to take a little break and get off my feet. We've been fairly swamped since about five o'clock. It seemed like everyone in the entire town decided to eat out tonight. Speaking of people in town, I heard through the grapevine that Forest Stevens moved away."

"Yeah, he found true love with Dr. Patience Forbes, the forensic anthropologist who was at the ranch examining the bones in the pit that were found. He moved with her to Oklahoma City a week ago." And every day of the past week, Dusty had missed the big cowboy who had been his best friend since he was a scrawny, homeless thirteen-year-old.

"Good for him," Trisha replied. "I hope they both get their happily-ever-after."

Ask her, a little voice niggled in the back of his brain. *For the first time in your life, step up and go after what you really want.* "Trisha, I was wondering if maybe tonight after your shift you'd like to go to the Watering Hole and have a drink with me?"

Her eyes widened and darkened and she quickly looked down at the tabletop. Dusty's heart sank into his boots. He should have known better. Why would a gorgeous woman like her be interested in a cowboy like him? Besides, he knew that plenty of other men had asked her out and she'd rejected all of them. Why would he be any different?

She was silent for a long moment and just when Dusty was about to tell her never mind, to forget that he'd even asked, she looked up at him. "I'm sorry, Dusty. I couldn't possibly go tonight. My son is with his babysitter and she's expecting me home right after work."

"No problem," he replied hurriedly. He was just grateful that he'd already eaten his dumpling and could now make a quick escape.

"Maybe I could work something out with her for tomorrow night after work." Her cheeks flushed a charming pink. "I mean, if you'd still want to."

"Sure, I'd love to," he said as his heart once again lifted buoyantly in his chest.

"I work until ten tomorrow night. I could meet you at the Watering Hole around ten thirty or so."

He sat up straighter and smiled at her. "That sounds perfect. Why don't I give you my cell phone number in case it doesn't work out with your babysitter?" He grabbed a napkin and then used her pen to write down his number, and she wrote hers down for him, as well.

She scooted out of the booth, took the napkin with his number from him and stuffed it into her back pocket. "Then I guess I'll see you tomorrow night." She tore his tab off her ordering pad, slid it onto the table and then scurried away from the booth.

A wave of excitement swept through him. He'd done it. He'd not only gotten up the nerve to finally ask her out, but she'd actually accepted. He got up and walked to the cash register, where the owner of the café, Daisy Martin, greeted him with a wide grin.

"I saw you passing notes with Trisha. Are you trying to make time with one of my best waitresses?" she asked.

"Definitely trying to," he replied. He handed her a twenty-dollar bill.

Daisy's smile fell and she glanced over to Trisha, who was pouring coffee for the three men from the Humes ranch. She looked back at Dusty. "I hope you have the right intentions where she's concerned. She's a good woman and she deserves only the very best."

"Daisy, I didn't know you were such a protective mama bear," he said teasingly as he tucked his change into his back pocket.

Daisy swept a strand of her flaming red hair behind an ear. "I am when it comes to the girls who work for me. They're closer to me than most of my family."

"You don't have to worry about me, Daisy. Besides, I didn't ask her to jump into my bed or anything like that. I just asked her to have drinks at the Watering Hole with me," Dusty replied.

"Whatever—you just make sure you treat her right. Like I said before, she deserves only the best."

Minutes later Dusty was in his truck and headed back to the Holiday ranch. There was no question that he was eager to spend some time with Trisha away from her work. He'd been drawn to her for a long time. But he couldn't help thinking about what Daisy had said, that Trisha was a good woman who deserved only the best.

You're nothing but a sniveling punk.

The very sight of you makes me sick to my stomach.

You'll never amount to anything.

The hurtful words exploded in Dusty's head and he gripped the steering wheel more tightly as he battled to shove the deep, gravelly voice back into his past where it belonged.

It's just drinks, he reminded himself. He certainly hadn't proclaimed his undying love for Trisha. He didn't know what his intentions were toward the attractive woman. He didn't know her well enough yet.

The truth of the matter was that he didn't know if he was strong enough, smart enough or good enough to be with a woman like Trisha.

He reached up and touched his left ear, where he hadn't heard a sound since he was thirteen and had climbed out of a bedroom window to escape the man he'd feared would eventually kill him.

Nobody, not even his best friend, Forest, knew that Dusty was deaf in one ear.

He knew with confidence that he was a good cowboy. Cass Holiday had seen to that. But Cass was dead now, and Dusty was left with the sinking feeling that he really wasn't good enough for any woman.

It was just after ten o'clock when Trisha got into her car and headed to the Bitterroot Motel, where she and her son had been living for a little over two and a half years.

As she drove the short distance, her thoughts were filled with the cowboy who had asked her to have drinks with him.

There was no question that she was physically attracted to Dusty Crawford. He had hair the color of sun-kissed wheat and eyes the hue of a cobalt bottle.

Deep dimples flashed charmingly with his smiles that warmed her as no other man's had in a very long time.

They'd chatted often enough at the café that she knew she also liked his sunny disposition and easygoing attitude. Despite their interactions at her workplace, she only knew him superficially, and an excitement she hadn't felt in a very long time fluttered inside her at the thought of finally getting to know him better.

Is it safe?

Has enough time passed?

The troubling questions flew into her head unbidden and sent a new tension churning in the pit of her stomach. Surely after a little over three long years she was finally safe here and didn't have to worry about her past reaching out to torture her or anyone else ever again. Surely it was finally safe for her to believe that a happy future was possible for her and her son.

Any disturbing thoughts she might have momentarily entertained disappeared as she pulled up in front of unit 4 at the motel. The units were small but also had full kitchenettes, and the weekly rent was low enough that between her wages and her tips she'd been able to sock away some savings.

Still, she knew it was past time to make a move. It wasn't right to be raising a three-year-old little boy in the confines of a motel room. She was hoping that in the next couple of weeks or so she would find a small house to rent, a house where Cooper could play in the yard and have his very own room.

With thoughts of her son filling her heart, she left

her car and hurried toward the motel room door. She unlocked and opened it to see Juanita in the chair next to the bed where Cooper slept soundly. Juanita closed the tabloid she'd been reading and got out of the chair.

She joined Trisha at the door. "As usual he was a good boy today," she said softly. "We played outside on the swing set and then spent the hot hours of the afternoon playing games and watching movies inside. He ate a good dinner and then took a bath before he went to bed."

"Thanks, Juanita. I was wondering if maybe tomorrow night you could stay a little later than usual. Maybe until around midnight?"

Juanita's broad face wreathed in a smile and one of her thick dark eyebrows danced upward. "Does Cinderella have a ball to attend?"

Trisha bit back a laugh. "No, nothing quite as elegant as that…just drinks with a cowboy."

"And who is this lucky cowboy?"

"Dusty Crawford from the Holiday ranch."

Juanita quickly made the sign of the cross over her chest. "Something evil walked on that land."

Trisha knew she was referring to the seven skeletons that had been found on the property…skeletons who had once been young men who had been murdered over a decade ago.

"Hopefully, Chief of Police Bowie will find out who was responsible for that evil," Trisha replied.

Juanita nodded soberly and then smiled once again. "Staying late tomorrow night is no problem. It's about time you did something for yourself."

"Thanks, Juanita. I don't know what I would do without you. Now, go home and I'll see you tomorrow afternoon."

Trisha watched from the doorway as the older woman got into her car and then left the motel parking lot. Juanita Gomez had been a godsend since Trisha had begun working at the café.

The older Hispanic woman had lost her husband five years before to a heart attack, and with all of her children grown and living in different towns, Juanita had suffered from empty-nest and had wanted a babysitting job.

She was a kind, loving person and Trisha was grateful to have her taking care of her son. She closed and locked the motel room door and then gazed at the little boy in the king-size bed.

Cooper's white-blond hair was in boyish disarray, reminding her that he was way overdue for a haircut. A small smile curved his lips, as if his dreams were good ones. She hoped he always had wonderful dreams. He was her heart and soul and she would do anything necessary to keep him happy and safe.

She went into the bathroom and stripped off her clothes and threw them into a hamper. It took her a few minutes to take a quick shower and then change into a clean nightshirt.

It was only when she was in bed in the dark room that her thoughts once again filled with Dusty Crawford. During her time working as a waitress, plenty of men had asked her out and she'd always declined the offers.

But as much as Cooper filled her life, over the past couple of months she'd found herself hungering for something more. Dusty had always created a little sizzle of electricity in her.

Was he the right man for the rest of her life? She couldn't know for sure. What she did know was that he was the right man at the right time to ask her out tonight.

Is it safe?

The three words thundered in her brain. She squeezed her eyes tightly shut and shoved away the fear that tried to take hold of her.

She'd lived in fear for the past three years. Surely she could finally let go of it now. Surely after all this time, after all the measures she'd taken, she wasn't in any danger anymore.

With a tentative hope for a brighter future, she drifted off into a dreamless sleep. She awakened to little hands on either side of her face. "Mommy, it's time to wake up."

Trisha opened her eyes and gazed into the beautiful blue eyes of her son. "Says who?"

"Says Cooper!" he exclaimed.

"Cooper who?"

"Cooper Cahill."

It was a silly conversation they had almost every morning when he awakened her. She sat up and grinned at him. "And the tickle bug is about to attack Cooper Cahill." She proceeded to tickle Cooper until his childish giggles filled the room where the early morning sun drifted in around the edges of the gold curtains at the window.

Minutes later the scent of freshly brewed coffee filled the air and Cooper sat at the small kitchen table eating a bowl of cereal. Between bites he told her everything he wanted to do before she went to work at two that afternoon.

"We can swing and then we can play cowboys. You can be a bad guy and I'll be a good guy."

"Why do I always have to be the bad guy?" Trisha asked in amusement.

"'Cause I'm always a good guy," Cooper replied as if that made perfect sense.

Thankfully, the only bad guys Cooper knew were little action-figure cowboys he deemed to be bank robbers and cattle rustlers. She could only hope that he would never know the kind of true evil she'd once experienced.

The morning passed far too quickly as she and Cooper played outside on the motel playground and then moved inside when the heat of the day began to build. As usual when they played cowboys, his good guys put her bad guys in jail.

At one thirty Trisha donned a clean pair of jeans and the red T-shirt that identified her as one of the waitresses at the Bitterroot Café. She then stared into the closet at her meager wardrobe.

New clothes for herself hadn't been a priority over the past couple of years. She joyously bought for Cooper, but she'd rather tuck any spare money away in her savings fund to get them out of this motel room than buy anything new for herself.

She finally pulled out a royal blue sleeveless cotton blouse to change into later that night for her date with Dusty. She knew the blouse fit her well and brought out the color of her eyes.

She'd managed to get through the morning and early afternoon without thinking about meeting him after work for drinks, but now doubts began to plague her.

The doubts continued and followed her into work. Maybe she should just call him and cancel, she thought as she took dinner orders. What had sounded like a nice idea the night before now filled her with a nervous energy.

You deserve to spend some time with a handsome man who makes your heart flutter more than a little bit, she told herself firmly. *Even Juanita said you deserved it. It's only one night...a couple of hours at the most.*

Luckily, on a Saturday night, the dinner rush was busy enough that she didn't have much time to focus on her warring thoughts where meeting Dusty was concerned.

It was just after six o'clock when Zeke Osmond, Greg Albertson and Lloyd Green walked through the door and grabbed a booth in her section. Trisha swallowed a sigh.

She hated waiting on these men, who were not only rude and often lewd, but also pigs who didn't tip worth a darn. Greg wasn't too bad, but both Zeke and Lloyd made her skin crawl.

She gripped her order pad tightly in her hand and walked over to the booth were they were seated. "Good evening, gentlemen. What can I get for you all?"

"Trisha, honey, if you were on the menu I'd order you up in a hot minute," Zeke said, his dark eyes gliding over her from head to toe. "In fact, I'd make it a double order to go."

Lloyd elbowed his younger buddy and offered Trisha an apologetic smile that didn't quite meet his eyes. "Don't pay any attention to him, Trisha. You know he's just a dumb knucklehead."

Daisy ambled over to the booth and smiled at Trisha. "Trisha, why don't you go ahead and take your break now? I'll take care of these rascals."

With a sigh of relief, Trisha headed for the break room in the back of the café. Once inside the small room, she sat in one of the chairs and stared at her blouse hanging on a nearby coatrack. She pulled her cell phone from her pocket and gazed down at the keypad.

She'd already put Dusty's phone number into her list of contacts. All she had to do was punch a couple of buttons and she would be connected to him.

Desire battled with the old fear that had become so familiar. Was she a complete fool to believe that she could really have a normal life? A life that included going on dates with handsome cowboys and hopefully someday finding a special man who would love not only her but also her son?

She slid her phone back into her pocket. She wasn't going to cancel meeting Dusty. She had no idea if he might be that special man, but she'd never know if she didn't take a chance.

Is it safe?

She could only hope that she was truly free of the evil of her past.

Chapter 2

Dusty stood in front of the mirror above the sink in his tiny bathroom and gazed at his reflection. Hair neatly combed…check. Light blue dress shirt buttoned and tucked into his jeans…check.

He grabbed a bottle of spicy cologne and splashed it on both sides of his neck and beneath his jaw and then left the bathroom. He was ready ridiculously early. It was only a few minutes before nine.

Nerves bounced around in the pit of his stomach. He'd drive himself crazy if he cooled his heels alone in the small bunk room he called home.

He stepped out the door and gazed down the length of the motel-like units where the cowboys who worked on the Holiday ranch lived. None of the other men were anywhere in sight.

He began the walk around to the back of the building where the cowboy dining room and a recreation area were located. Most of the men would be in town on a Saturday night, but there were always a few who preferred hanging out together in the rec room.

"Whoa, we could smell you coming from a mile away," Adam Benson, the ranch foreman, exclaimed as he waved a hand in front of his nose when Dusty walked in.

"And he's nice and cleaned up, too," Tony Nakni, another ranch hand, added. "Hot date?"

"I don't know how hot it's going to be, but I'm meeting Trisha at the Watering Hole after she gets off work at the café," Dusty said and sank down on a chair next to Tony.

Tony clapped him on the back. "So, you finally got up the nerve to ask her out."

"Yeah, and even more surprising is that she actually agreed to meet with me." Nerves once again kicked up in the pit of Dusty's stomach.

"Well, it's about time," Adam replied. "You've been half-crazy about her forever."

"You're one to talk. Everyone knows you have a thing for Cassie. When are you going to ask her out on an official date?" Dusty asked.

Cassie Peterson had inherited the ranch from her aunt Cass, the woman who had taken in a bunch of dysfunctional, lost young boys and turned them into not just cowboys, but also strong and capable men.

There had been a lot of speculation as to whether the pretty blonde would stay and work the ranch or sell it and return to New York City, where she had a store that sold her original oil paintings, among other things.

The crime scene that had been discovered on the property had temporarily halted any plans she might have entertained of selling the ranch, but none of them knew what Cassie's next move might be now that the skeletons had been removed.

"Yeah, maybe if you cozied up to her a little bit more then you could convince her to stick around here," Tony said to Adam.

"You all know that the last thing I want is for her to sell out and leave us all not only jobless but homeless and separated, as well," Adam replied.

They were all silent for a long moment. With the help of social worker Francine Rogers, Cass Holiday had taken in a dozen runaway boys to work her ranch. As they'd grown and matured, they had formed a family unit and Dusty had considered each one of the other men a brother.

As the others continued to speculate on Cassie's future plans for the ranch, Dusty was far more concerned about his own imminent future and his date with Trisha.

He'd dated several women in town over the past couple of years, but he'd never made a real connection with any of them. Sometimes he wondered in the darkness of the night if his childhood had made it impossible for him to ever trust...to ever really love anyone.

He remained talking with the other men until nine

thirty and then stood. "It's time for me to head out," he said.

"Good luck," Tony said. "I hope you both have a great time."

"Don't do anything I wouldn't do," Adam added.

Dusty laughed. "I wouldn't think of it."

He left the building and headed for the large shed where the men parked their personal vehicles and stored other big ranch equipment.

In the brilliant moonlight, the blue tent that covered the crime scene rose up like an alien entity. He grimaced as he thought of the skeletons. They had been found under the floorboards of an old shed the men had taken down after the spring storm that had killed Cass.

The discovery had been shocking, and even more shocking was that Chief of Police Dillon Bowie suspected it was possible that one of the men working the ranch might be responsible for the seven murdered young men.

Dusty would never believe that one of the men he considered his brothers was responsible for the murders that had occurred around the time the twelve young men had first begun working for Cass.

She had been a good judge of character and surely never would have kept anyone around who showed any kind of violent tendencies, somebody who was capable of slamming a meat cleaver or an ax into the skull of another human being.

If there was a killer in Bitterroot, then the odds were much better that he worked on the Humes ranch.

Raymond Humes liked his ranch hands mean and on the edge, and many of them had been around for years or had been born and raised here.

As Dusty drove the short distance from the ranch into town, all thoughts of the murders fled his mind as he once again thought about the night to come with Trisha.

He had no idea if she was a potential long-term match for him or not. All he knew for sure was that he was attracted to her. For months she had invaded his thoughts and dreams. There was also a growing well of loneliness deep inside him.

Maybe his loneliness was more apparent lately because three of his fellow cowboys had found their love matches in the last couple of months. They had been a dozen single men working and living together, and now they were only nine. Dusty wanted to find the same kind of happiness that they had all found.

The Watering Hole was the only official bar in town. It was housed in a large wooden building and on a Saturday night the parking lot was nearly full.

He wished that there had been someplace to meet that was a little quieter, but this was basically the only game in town at this time of the night other than the café where Trisha worked.

Hopefully, he could snag a table away from the dance floor, where the music would be softer and they could actually carry on some kind of a meaningful conversation without too much difficulty.

He found an empty parking space and pulled in. The dog days of August were upon them. The stifling night air slapped him in the face as he hurried from his pickup toward the cooler air that would greet him inside the bar.

The place was definitely jumping. Dozens of couples moved across the dance floor to the beat of the jukebox playing a rousing country western song. Bottles and glasses clinked as drinks were poured and delivered by the waitresses, and laughter rang out from all four corners of the huge room.

Dusty waved to Brody Booth, Sawyer Quincy and Jerrod Steen, all fellow cowboys from the Holiday ranch. They sat together at a table near the back room, where there were two pool tables and a dartboard.

Dusty smiled inwardly. It was a good thing Brody and Jerrod were with Sawyer. The copper-haired cowboy was a lightweight when it came to drinking. It didn't take much beer for him to have to be carried out of the place.

Dusty wove his way through the crowd and spied an empty two-top table not far from where the three men sat. At least the jukebox wasn't quite as loud here, although the noisy click of pool balls and triumphant shouts drifted out of the back room.

He sat and once again tamped down the nerves that kicked in the pit of his stomach. He had never been so nervous before meeting or picking up any woman for a date.

It was just drinks, he reminded himself. If they weren't into each other by the end of the night, they would each go their own separate ways and there would be no harm and no foul.

"Hey, Dusty." Janis Little, one of the waitresses, greeted him with a friendly smile. "What can I get for you?"

Dusty looked at his watch. It was just ten minutes after ten. Trisha should be arriving within the next fifteen minutes or so. "I'll have a beer," he said. "But I'm waiting for Trisha Cahill to join me in the next few minutes."

Janis raised one of her thin brown eyebrows. "Ah, and here I thought your heart belonged only to me."

He grinned at the attractive woman. "You know I have to keep up my appearances as a womanizing cowboy who secretly loves and trusts only my horse."

She laughed. "I'll be back with your beer in a jiffy."

He watched her as she worked her way toward the long, polished bar on the opposite side of the room. Janis was pretty and single, but he'd never considered asking her out. She'd never created the edge of excitement in him that Trisha did.

Janis delivered his beer and he'd only taken two sips of it when Trisha walked through the front door. He immediately jumped to his feet and waved to her.

She smiled and waved back. He remained standing as she went around the tables and people to approach him. His heart quickened as she drew nearer. She looked ridiculously hot. Her pale blond hair was loose and flowed to her shoulders in soft waves. Her tight jeans showcased her long, slim legs and the blue blouse skimmed her full breasts and tapered in at her slender waist.

"Trisha, I'm so glad you could make it," he said when she finally reached the table.

"Me, too." Only after she sat at the table did Dusty return to his chair opposite of her.

Was she as nervous as he was? She didn't appear to be. She looked cool and collected. "What can I get for you?" he asked and motioned to Janis.

"I really don't drink too often, but a beer sounds wonderful. It's so hot outside."

"There's nothing better than a cold beer on a hot summer night," he replied.

"We'll be wishing for these hot nights when the snow starts to fly."

Janis arrived and took the drink order, and once it had been delivered the conversation turned to Trisha's night working at the café. "Saturday nights are always the worst," she said. "I swear nobody in the entire town cooks on Saturday nights." She gave him a rueful grin. "Oh, wait, didn't I say that to you last night about Friday nights?"

"I believe you did. But that's small-town living. Weekend meals aren't just about the food, but also about community ties and, of course, the gossip," he replied dryly.

She laughed, a pleasant, musical sound. "That's for sure," she agreed. "I now know more personal information about some of the people in this town than I ever wanted to know." She sobered slightly. "And despite how good the gossip mill is and that you and I have talked fairly regularly at the café, I really don't know that much about you. Did you grow up here in Bitterroot?"

"No, I'm a transplant. I grew up in Oklahoma City. What about you? Where are you from originally?" The last thing he wanted to talk about was himself and his past.

"I'm from back east," she replied and took a drink of her beer.

"Then how did you wind up here in Bitterroot?" he asked curiously. He was aware that her answer had definitely been vague. *Back east* could include a million different places when you lived in Oklahoma.

She gazed down into her glass and then looked at him once again. The blue of her eyes was slightly darker than a moment before.

"When I was three months pregnant, my boyfriend, the father of my unborn child, was killed in a terrible motorcycle accident. When my son was born, I decided that I needed a fresh start, someplace new. So, I packed up my bags and my baby and took off."

"Wow, that was incredibly brave of you," he replied.

She smiled and picked up her glass once again. "I don't know if it was incredibly brave or completely foolish, but at the time I knew it was definitely what I needed to do. I spent the next six months or so drifting from town to town, and finally we wound up here in Bitterroot. So far it's been a good fit."

She took another drink of her beer and when she set her glass back on the table, Dusty noticed that her hand trembled slightly and her gaze went to some point just over his head.

Interesting, he mused inwardly. Were her hands simply trembling from the nerves of a first date? Or was it something more?

Rather than being put off, he was more intrigued by her than ever. He certainly didn't know her well at this point, but he had the distinct impression that Trisha Cahill just might have a barn full of secrets.

Trisha fought against the ghosts from her past and the fact that she was telling lies. They left a bad taste in her mouth. She didn't want to lie, but she had to. It was far too early to bare her soul to Dusty. Besides, she'd never hope to have a normal life if she told the truth and chased anyone who might be interested in her away.

"I know you have a young son. Tell me about him," Dusty said.

Instantly the nerves that had danced inside her as she'd talked briefly about how she'd come to be here in Bitterroot calmed. "Cooper is a little over three years old and he's the absolute love of my life. He adores blueberry pancakes and playing cowboys and old John Wayne movies."

Dusty laughed and raised a blond eyebrow. "Really? Old John Wayne movies?"

She nodded and grinned. "The motel doesn't get many television channels, but one of them plays old Westerns, and Cooper has already decided he's going to be the cowboy who arrests all of the bad guys and saves the town just like the Duke."

"He sounds pretty special."

"Oh, he is…of course I might be slightly prejudiced."

"Mothers are supposed to be prejudiced when it comes to their children," he replied firmly. "What about other family?"

"None," she replied. "I'm an only child, and my father passed away when I was in high school and my mother died when I was pregnant with Cooper." She ignored the pang of guilt…the pain of enormous grief that shot off in her stomach and filled her heart.

"I'm sorry to hear that," he said with genuine empathy shining from his gorgeous eyes. "That's something we have in common. I don't have any family, either."

For the next hour or so the conversation flowed comfortably between them. With each minute that passed she found herself drawn to him more and more.

Not only did she find him crazy handsome and sexy, but he was also easy to talk to and had a wonderful sense of humor. Thankfully she managed to steer the conversation away from her and focused on him and his work at the Holiday ranch.

He talked about his fellow cowboys and regaled her with stories about them that brought laughter to her lips again and again. It felt good not just to have something to laugh about but also to see the warmth in his eyes as he gazed at her, to feel the tingling excitement of her incredible attraction to him.

It was just a little after eleven thirty when he asked her if she wanted to take a whirl out on the dance floor. The jukebox had begun to play a slow song and she suddenly wanted to know what it would feel like to have his big, strong arms around her. It had been so long since she'd been held by anyone.

"Okay," she agreed. "Although I have to warn you that it's been years since I've danced with anyone, so I'm sure I'm pretty rusty."

"I'll take rusty anytime," he said with a charming smile and jumped up from his chair. She also stood and he took her by the hand and led her toward the edge of the dance floor, where other couples clung together and danced to the music.

With one hand at her waist and the other one holding her hand, he pulled her to within an inch or so of his body and they began to move to the slow beat.

His shoulder was big and strong beneath her hand and the clean male scent of him coupled with a spicy cologne threatened to dizzy her senses. He led with confidence and moved with an unexpected grace for a cowboy.

This short night had only confirmed what she had suspected for months...that she was ridiculously drawn to Dusty Crawford. It wasn't just because she could drown in the depths of his beautiful blue eyes or because the flash of his dimples warmed her deep inside. It wasn't that he had a sexy taut butt and shoulders that appeared wide enough to carry any burden.

She was also drawn to the man she sensed he was beneath his handsome outer wrapping. There was a warmth to him, and an aura of a good man with a big heart.

She was vaguely disappointed when the music finally ended because she knew it was time for her to call an end to the night and head back to the motel. She'd told Juanita that she'd be home by midnight, and no matter how much she was enjoying herself she wouldn't take advantage of the situation by being late.

They walked back to the table, but she didn't return to her chair. She picked up her purse from the floor beneath the table. "I'm sorry, Dusty, but I really need to get going," she said.

A flash of disappointment shone from his eyes. It was there only a moment and then gone. "I'm sorry, too, but I understand. Just let me pay for the tab and I'll follow you home."

"Oh, that isn't necessary," she protested.

He waved to Janis. "But it is necessary," he replied. "A real gentleman always sees a lady home safely."

A wealth of unexpected emotion welled up inside her. It had been a very long time since any man had wanted to see her safely anywhere.

He paid for their drinks and then the two of them left the bar and stepped out into the warmth of the night. "I'll be right behind you," he said when they reached her car. "We can say our final good-nights at your door."

Minutes later she glanced in her rearview mirror

and was oddly comforted by the lights of his bright red pickup truck just behind her.

The night had been far too short. Would he ask her out again? Did he even want to spend more time with her? She was surprised by how much she wanted him to.

Would he kiss her? A fluttering shot off in the pit of her stomach. Goodness, she felt like a silly schoolgirl with her very first crush.

She parked her car in front of her motel unit and Dusty pulled his truck up just behind her car. Before she had shut off her engine he was at her door.

She turned off her car and unfastened her seat belt as he opened the door for her. He stepped aside to allow her to get out.

"Trisha, I really enjoyed spending time with you tonight." The neon lights from the motel sign flickered red and yellow on his strong, handsome features.

"I enjoyed it, too," she replied. Her heart beat a little faster as he took a step closer to her.

"I'd like to spend more time with you. Does your son like to fish?"

She looked at him in surprise. "He's never been fishing before, but I'm sure he'd love it."

"Then what if we plan a day of the two of you coming out to the ranch? We can do a little fishing in the pond and maybe have a picnic?"

Her head told her it was far too soon to introduce Cooper to Dusty, and yet as she thought of her son enjoying a day outside and learning how to fish, she couldn't resist the invitation. Besides, it wasn't as if she'd just met Dusty. She tamped down any reservations she might have. "That sounds like fun."

He took another step toward her. "When is your next day off?"

"Tomorrow." Once again the fluttering was back in her stomach.

"Then can we plan it for around three tomorrow afternoon? I can pick the two of you up here and I'll arrange it all so you don't have to do a thing."

"That would be wonderful," she replied.

His eyes glittered with pleasure. "Then it's a date. And now, the most important question of the evening. Can I kiss you good-night?"

She was surprised that he'd asked her and even more surprised by just how badly she wanted him to kiss her. "Yes, I'd like that."

She barely got the words out of her mouth before he took her into his arms. Unlike when they had danced, this time there was no space between them. She was acutely conscious of his firm, muscled body against hers as he lowered his head to capture her lips with his.

Soft and warm, he moved his mouth against hers. Fire leaped into her veins and she wrapped her arms around his neck. She parted her lips to allow him to deepen the kiss and he did, his tongue swirling with hers.

What had begun as a simple, soft first kiss quickly flared into something hotter, something far more intense than she had initially anticipated.

Reluctantly, she pulled her arms from around his

neck and broke the kiss. He immediately dropped his arms to his sides and stepped back from her. "Whew," he said with a grin.

She gave a breathy laugh. "I second that. And now I really should get inside." She had to escape before she lost her head and threw herself into his arms once again for another kiss…and another.

They had only taken a couple of steps toward her motel room door when she spied something odd. Directly in front of her door on the ground was a bright yellow coffee mug with a little bouquet of wildflowers spilling out of the top.

A wail began in the center of her brain and she froze, unable to think, unable to even move as a distant but familiar terror rocketed through her.

"What's this?" Dusty's voice slowly penetrated into her head. She stared wordlessly as he bent down and picked up the mug. "It looks like there's a note, too." He retrieved a white piece of paper that had been tucked beneath the mug.

He held the paper out to her. With trembling fingers she took it from him. Her mouth was dry with fear as she opened it. In the light from the blinking neon motel sign and the bright moon overhead, the words written in red marker practically leaped off the page: "YOU BELONG TO ME."

Horror clutched her throat, momentarily closing it off so that she could scarcely draw a breath of air. *No*, her mind screamed. *No, please.*

Is it safe? It isn't. Dear God, it isn't safe at all.

"I've got to go. I need to pack up and leave town.

We need to get out of here." The words fell from her lips as she continued to stare at Dusty.

"Whoa." He set the mug down on the ground next to him and reached out and grabbed her by her shoulders. "Trisha, slow down. I think maybe you're over-reacting. I'm the one who should be worried here. It appears that you have a secret admirer and I have some competition."

A secret admirer?

Was that all that it was?

She tried to staunch the sheer terror that had momentarily clutched at her very soul. Was she really overreacting? She continued to stare at Dusty and then looked down at the mug on the ground next to her.

"Trisha, are you all right?" Dusty asked with concern.

A touch of embarrassment swept over her and she gazed up at him once again. "I'm fine. I…I just don't like surprises."

"This surprise just makes me wish I'd thought to bring you a dozen roses," he said dryly. He dropped his hands from her shoulders.

She drew in a deep, steadying breath. "Dusty, I don't need roses, or flowers in a coffee mug from an unknown person."

"Then we're still on for our fishing date tomorrow?"

"Of course we're still on," she replied. "Would you do me a favor?" She crumpled up the note into a tight ball and shoved it into his hand. "Would you throw this and the mug into the Dumpster for me?"

"Are you sure? The flowers are kind of pretty."

"I'm positive. I don't want them. Like I said, I don't like surprises."

"Then it would be my pleasure." He reached down and picked up the mug and then frowned at her with concern. "Are you sure you're okay?"

"I'm fine." All she wanted to do now was get into the motel room.

"Then I'll just say good-night, Trisha."

She murmured a good-night and then escaped into her room. She held it together as she told Juanita good-night. She even managed to remain somewhat calm as she went into the bathroom and changed into her nightshirt.

It was only then that the fear returned and once again sizzled inside her. She walked to the window and moved the heavy gold curtain aside just enough that she could peek outside.

Who on earth had left the note and the flowers for her? Was there somebody out there watching her right now? The parking lot appeared empty of any human presence, but there were so many places to hide.

The large trash Dumpster at the back of the parking lot now looked like a perfect place for somebody to conceal himself from her view. The line of mature trees and thick bushes appeared equally malevolent in the darkness of the night.

A secret admirer? Who could it be?

She let the curtain fall back into place and checked

the door, making sure that both the dead bolt and the security chain were in place.

She finally slid into the king-size bed next to her sleeping son. She stared up at the dark ceiling, her thoughts racing a hundred miles a minute.

Was it safe? There had never been any notes or flowers before. Were they really just the result of some lonesome cowboy or some man in town who had developed a crush on her? Were they from a harmless secret admirer, as Dusty had suggested?

Squeezing her eyes tightly closed, she tried to still the frantic race of her heart. She didn't want to pack up her things and run again. She loved living in Bitterroot and tonight with Dusty had been all kinds of wonderful.

Did she take the chance and stay here in town and see what happened next? Was this nothing to be afraid of, or had the evil from her past finally caught up with her?

Chapter 3

Sundays at the Holiday ranch were fairly laid-back. The chores were divided so that half of the men worked one Sunday and the others were off, and the next weekend the men who'd been off worked. The system assured that every other week the men got a full day off without having to do any of the daily chores required to keep the ranch running smoothly.

Thankfully, it was Dusty's turn to have the entire day off. He slept later than usual but was still up not long after dawn. His first thought when he awakened was of Trisha and the time he'd shared with her the night before.

Bright and fun, she'd been everything he'd dreamed about and more. She'd been so easy to talk to and with each minute that had passed he'd only grown more attracted to her.

As he showered his thoughts continued to be consumed by his date with her. He'd loved the way she'd felt in his arms as they'd danced, and kissing her had been nothing short of amazing.

But the night had definitely turned a little strange when she'd seen the note and the flowers that had been left for her at the motel door. Her initial reaction had seemed a little bit over-the-top with her saying that she needed to leave town and the crazy fear radiating from her wide blue eyes.

He wondered what might have happened to her in her past to cause her to react that way. He also wondered who in the hell had left the unexpected gifts for her. Someplace out there was a man trying to make time with her, too. Still, he knew that all he could do was focus on his own relationship with Trisha and see where things went from here.

He left his room and headed to the dining room, where breakfast would be in progress. As always, Cord Cully, aka Cookie, stood next to a long table where warming buffet servers held scrambled eggs, crispy strips of bacon and hot biscuits with sausage gravy. There was also fresh fruit and hearty oatmeal. Breakfast and dinner were the two big meals of the day, with lunch being lighter.

"Just the man I wanted to talk to," Dusty said to Cookie after he'd filled his plate and before he took a seat at one of the long picnic tables with the other men.

Cookie grunted, his dark eyes glowering as he

looked at Dusty. Dusty wasn't put off by Cookie's countenance. The man looked as if he wanted to punch something most of the time. "Talk to me about what?"

"A picnic lunch." Dusty quickly told the man what he wanted for later that afternoon. When he was finished, Tony Nakni motioned for Dusty to sit beside him.

Tony was half Choctaw Indian and something of a mystery, although he and Dusty had always shared a good relationship. "How did it go last night?" he asked once Dusty had gotten settled.

"Really good," Dusty replied. "In fact, we're having a picnic down by the pond this afternoon and I'm going to teach her three-year-old son, Cooper, how to fish."

Tony raised a dark brow. "You must have made a good impression on her if she's letting you meet her son already."

"I hope I made a good impression, because it appears that I have a little competition." He told Tony about the note and the flowers.

Tony shook his head. "I've never understood that kind of approach. I mean, if you want a woman, then don't play silly games, just go after her."

Dusty looked at his friend in open amusement. "And exactly when are you going to decide to go after a woman?"

"When and if I ever find somebody worth pursuing," Tony replied.

The dining room suddenly fell silent. Dusty looked up to see that Cassie Peterson stood in the doorway.

She was clad in a pair of designer jeans and a bright pink blouse and her blond hair looked as if it had been styled by a professional hairdresser only minutes before. She was definitely a little bit of big city in the room.

It was rarely a good thing when she appeared in the cowboy dining area, especially first thing in the morning.

"I'm sorry to bother you all while you're eating breakfast," she said. "But I wanted to let you know that Chief Bowie is planning to interview you all again and I want you to make yourselves available to him. You all know how important it is to cooperate with him so that he can get answers as to the mystery of the skeletons that were found on the property."

"He's already interviewed us once," Brody Booth said.

"I'd like to know if he's looking at the ranch hands on the Humes ranch as carefully as he's looking at all of us," Flint McCay added.

Cassie held up her hands. "I'm sure Dillon is conducting interviews with everyone he thinks necessary to get to the bottom of the murders. Again, I would appreciate your cooperation in this matter. Thanks in advance."

"She probably wants this all cleared up so she can sell the ranch," Tony said darkly once Cassie had left the building. "I'm sure it would be hard to sell a ranch where seven unsolved murders took place."

"Raymond Humes would buy this place in a minute," Dusty said. "I heard that he's already contacted her about buying her out."

Tony's black eyes flashed with annoyance. "If she sells to him, then Cass's spirit will never rest peacefully. She hated that man."

Nobody knew what had happened between Raymond Humes and Cass Holiday that had created such bad blood between them. Dusty only knew that thoughts of the tough woman who had taken them all in still caused a piercing ache of loss deep in his heart.

A half an hour later, he left the dining area and went back to his room. He fought the impulse to call Trisha to make sure she really hadn't packed up her son and all of their belongings and left town sometime during the night. He still couldn't make sense of her dramatic reaction to the flowers and the note, but he hoped maybe when he saw her they would be able to have a conversation that would shed a little light on it.

In the meantime he had plenty of things to do to keep him busy until it was time for him to pick up her and her son for the afternoon of fun.

The last thing he wanted to do was entertain thoughts about the murders on this land and the fact that Dillon Bowie would interview him once again.

Dusty wasn't worried about having another conversation with the lawman. He had nothing to hide and he was certain that none of his brothers had anything to do with the horrendous crime that had taken place around the time they had all been brought to the ranch.

At just a little after nine o'clock, Dusty headed

into town. He wanted to pick up a few things so that the day with Trisha and her young son would be a complete success.

The first place he stopped was Bob's Bait Shack just off the main drag. The weathered wooden building held not only an array of hunting and fishing equipment, but also different kinds of bait.

He got what he needed for the afternoon fishing date and then headed to the café for a midmorning cup of coffee. He had a feeling that the hours were going to drag as anticipation and a touch of anxiety pooled inside him when he thought of Trisha.

Surely she would have called him by now if she'd done something crazy like packed up and left town, he thought as he entered the café.

"Hey, Dusty," Daisy greeted him and pointed him to an empty two-top, where Julia Hatfield took his order and then delivered his coffee.

Even if Trisha hadn't called him, surely she would have contacted Daisy by now to give her a heads-up if she was no longer going to work at the café. Daisy had said nothing to him about that happening when he'd come in.

He sipped his coffee and watched customers arrive and depart, and instead of thinking about Trisha, he found himself thinking about her son.

He'd never spent much time around kids. He certainly hadn't ever really considered whether he wanted children or not. He didn't know how to be a father. He definitely hadn't had a stellar role model where parents were concerned.

A knot of tension fisted up in his stomach and a phantom pain fired off in his left ear. He'd lied to Trisha when he'd told her he didn't have any family. As far as he knew his parents were still alive and well in Oklahoma City, but they'd both been dead to Dusty since he'd left home and them far behind.

He hadn't wanted to share any part of his nightmarish past with Trisha on their very first date.

Only Forest Stevens had known the full extent of what Dusty had gone through in his childhood. The big cowboy had been not only another runaway on the streets but had also become Dusty's best friend and protector during those dark and frightening days before they'd finally landed at Cass's ranch for a second chance at life.

Dusty knew in his very gut that he would have died on the streets without Forest watching over him. He mentally made a note to call his friend soon.

He was working on his second cup of coffee when Zeke Osmond walked into the café. The dark-haired, wiry man spied Dusty and immediately headed toward him. Dusty sat up straighter in his chair and wondered what Zeke might want with him. The two of them certainly didn't share any kind of a friendship.

"I heard through the grapevine that you were out with Trisha last night," he said as he stopped next to Dusty's chair. The man smelled of body odor, cigarette smoke and cow manure.

"You heard right," Dusty replied. "You have a problem with it?"

"I just didn't know that she was stupid enough to waste any of her time on a snot-nosed, no-account cowboy who had a social worker and a crazy old broad as his parents." Zeke rocked back on his heels and narrowed his eyes as if anticipating some kind of violent response.

Dusty wouldn't give him the pleasure despite the swift bite of anger that roared up in his chest. "Are you done here?" He held Zeke's gaze for a long moment and then looked down at the table and picked up his coffee cup, as if the man warranted not another second of his time or attention.

He sensed when Zeke walked away from the table and he looked up again to see the creep joining another group of men at a booth on the other side of the café.

Why on earth did Zeke Osmond give a damn about him seeing Trisha…unless Zeke wanted her for himself? Was it possible that Zeke was responsible for the mug of flowers and the note that had been left at her doorstep the night before?

Could Zeke be her secret admirer?

The very thought made Dusty slightly sick to his stomach. He didn't know if he was the man Trisha wanted or needed in her life, but he'd sure as hell do anything in his power to make sure somebody like Zeke didn't become that man.

It had been one of the longest nights of Trisha's life. She'd tossed and turned for hours as she'd wondered what she should do. Just after three in the morning, she finally made the decision to do nothing for now.

Once she'd decided to stay in Bitterroot and not immediately gather her things and leave, she'd fallen into a sleep tormented by nightmares of dead wild-flowers and a big, ominous shadow man chasing her through the night.

Cooper had awakened at his usual early time, and as he ate breakfast Trisha drank a cup of coffee and thought about the afternoon to come.

Despite her concern about the "gifts" that had been left for her, she was looking forward to spending more time with Dusty, which had ultimately made her decide to hang around.

Hopefully he'd been right when he'd immediately declared that she apparently had a secret admirer, and hopefully it was somebody from town and not a certain someone from her past.

Before she'd finally gone to sleep, a dozen names of men who could potentially be the mystery man had jumped into her brain. They were men who always chose to sit in her section when she was working at the café, or who had asked her out in the past. She supposed that any one of them could have left her the flowers and the note.

After breakfast as she and Cooper headed outside to the small motel playground, she shoved all thoughts of the troubling situation out of her head. She simply didn't want to think about it today.

"I've got a surprise for you," she said to her son as he took a seat on one of the faded red swings.

"A surprise?" His eyes lit up in anticipation.

"How would you like it if a cowboy picked us up this afternoon and took us fishing on the ranch where he works?"

Cooper's eyes widened. "A real cowboy and fishing?" He kicked his little legs with excitement. "What's the cowboy's name? Is it the Duke?"

Trisha laughed. "No, honey, it isn't the Duke. His name is Dusty and he's really nice."

"And he's gonna tell me how to catch a fish?" Once again Cooper wiggled in the swing seat with barely contained happiness. "I can't wait. I want to go now. When will he be here?"

"After your nap this afternoon," she replied. "Now, hang on tight so that I can give you a push."

Later that day when Cooper was napping, Trisha took a long shower and considered the fact that she was introducing her son to a man. She didn't know if it was a good idea or a bad one to introduce the two so quickly. She had no rule book to study to find the correct answer in this situation.

All she did know was that Cooper would love the plans for the day and it would be good for him to have a little male interaction.

Over the past couple of months he'd occasionally asked why he didn't have a daddy. She'd told her son the same lie that she had told Dusty—that his father had died in a tragic accident. She had no other choice, for the truth was so much worse than the lie. How did you tell a little boy that his daddy was a monster?

Besides, maybe it was a good thing to see how

Dusty interacted with Cooper right from the get-go. If Cooper didn't like Dusty, or she sensed that Dusty didn't like her son, then that would definitely be the end of things between them.

She dressed in a pair of jean shorts and a sleeveless denim blouse that had pearly white snaps up the front. She couldn't help the surge of excitement that winged through her as she anticipated spending more time with Dusty.

She wanted to let herself go, to be happy and carefree. Was that really too much to ask of life after all she'd endured in the past?

While Cooper continued his nap, she sat at the table and looked at the house rentals listed in the Bitterroot newspaper.

Today there were a total of five listed. The first two were too big and expensive. One was too far out of town, but the last two had promise. She circled the two ads with a red pen, determined to check them out within the next couple of days.

Although she'd told herself that she would make a move in the next month or two, as she gazed at her son sleeping in the center of the motel room bed they shared, she knew it was way past time that she found them a more permanent home. Cooper deserved so much better than the living conditions they had now.

She awakened Cooper at two. Normally if she woke him up before he got his complete nap, he was a little cranky bug. But today he got up with a huge smile on his face and cowboys and fishing on his mind.

She dressed him in a clean pair of jean shorts and

a red T-shirt and then slathered a liberal dose of sunscreen over any exposed skin. She topped his head with a red ball cap that would keep the sun off his tender scalp.

By two forty-five they were ready for Dusty's arrival. The only last-minute thing they would have to do was move Cooper's child seat from her car to Dusty's truck. Thankfully, he had a king cab and the seat could be easily fastened into his backseat.

"I see a red truck," Cooper exclaimed from his perch at the window. "Is that him, Mommy? Is that Dusty?"

"He has a red pickup truck, so that must be him," she replied as butterflies took wing in her stomach.

Cooper scrambled out of his chair at the window and raced to the motel room door. "Come on, it's time to go," he said exuberantly.

Trisha laughed with an exuberance of her own. She was determined not to think about any negative things for the rest of the day. She was just going to embrace spending time with a handsome cowboy and her beloved son.

Chief of Police Dillon Bowie had never been so frustrated in his thirty-five years of life as he'd been since the skeletal remains had been unearthed on the Holiday ranch.

August would soon become September and then October, and he couldn't imagine not having the heinous murders solved before the first snow began to fly.

The problem was that as good as Dr. Patience

Forbes had been when she'd removed and studied the bones, as efficient as the Oklahoma City crime lab had been in conducting all kinds of tests, nobody had come up with any real clues that could help in solving the crime that had taken place over a decade ago.

Even Francine Rogers, the social worker who had been responsible for bringing street kids to Cass Holiday for a second chance at life, hadn't been much help. Her old records were spotty, and at seventy-two years old her memory wasn't as good as it might have once been.

The one concrete piece of evidence that had come to light was a masculine gold ring with an onyx stone that had been found at the bottom of the burial pit. Dillon didn't know if it belonged to the killer or to one of the victims. He hadn't told anyone about the find. He preferred keeping it close to his chest for now.

What he did know was that the skeletons had belonged to boys between approximately fourteen and eighteen years old. One of the skeletons had been missing finger bones and another had been absent the skull.

All of the victims had been killed by a single blow to the back of the head with a sharp instrument. They hadn't been murdered all at the same time but rather over the course of several months.

Dillon got up from his desk and buckled on his gun belt. One thing was for sure, he wouldn't find the answers sitting in his office and stewing.

Although he had no real evidence to prove that the

person responsible for the murders was still in the town he served, his gut told him otherwise.

Something bad had happened on the Holiday ranch years ago around the time when the cowboys who now worked and lived there had first arrived to begin their new lives.

Despite his attraction to new owner Cassie Peterson, his number-one job was to make sure that she wasn't unknowingly harboring a man capable of such evil.

Chapter 4

Dusty had just gotten out of his truck when the motel room door flew open and a pint-size little boy in jeans and a red T-shirt and ball cap came barreling out with Trisha just behind him.

"Howdy, partner," he said to Dusty in a surprisingly deep voice.

"Howdy. You must be Cooper. My name is Dusty."

Cooper grinned, his blue eyes so like his mother's and sparkling with obvious excitement. "I know, and you're going to take us fishing." His voice was no longer deep, letting Dusty know that his initial greeting was probably his idea of a John Wayne imitation.

"Hi, Dusty," Trisha said. "I guess I don't have to make official introductions between the two of you."

Dusty grinned at the little boy and then looked back at Trisha. "I think we're good, right, Cooper?"

"We're good," Cooper echoed. "Let's go."

It took several minutes to actually get going as Dusty transferred the child seat from her car to the backseat of his truck. Finally, they were all buckled in and on their way.

"I'm going to catch a great big fish," Cooper said. "Maybe even a whale."

Dusty exchanged a glance of amusement with Trisha. "I don't think you'll find any whales in the pond, but you might manage to catch a big old catfish."

"A catfish? Do they meow? I can meow." Cooper proceeded to make cat sounds. "I can bark, too. You want to hear me bark, Dusty? I bark real good."

"Honey, you might want to keep the animals all quiet for now," Trisha said.

Once again Dusty shot a quick glance in her direction. She looked as amazing as he'd ever seen her. She was definitely born to wear denim. Her eyes had taken on the hue of her blouse and her shorts displayed long shapely legs.

Her hair sparkled in the sunshine and was caught up in a ponytail that emphasized the delicate bone structure of her lovely face.

A wave of heat rushed over him as he thought about the kiss they had shared the night before. As much as Dusty wanted to taste her lips once again, there would be no kisses today, not with Cooper present. This afternoon wasn't just about the two of them, but rather the three of them.

Cooper kept up a steady stream of chatter on the short drive from the motel to the ranch. He asked a hundred questions of both Dusty and his mom.

Dusty certainly didn't know anything about three-year-olds, but he was surprised by how bright Cooper appeared, how eager he was to learn things. *Why* was definitely one of his favorite words as he asked why trees grew up and why did cows have four legs? These were among other questions of seemingly great importance to Cooper.

When they reached the ranch, Dusty parked his truck in the shed and then they all transferred to one of the motorized carts that were used occasionally to get around the place without horses.

Trisha sat in the passenger seat with Cooper in her lap and Dusty took off for the cowboy dining room to retrieve the picnic food Cookie had prepared for them.

"I've already got the fishing equipment down by the pond," he said as he drove slowly, aware of his precious cargo. "We just need to stop and pick up the food."

"Mommy and I had a picnic once at the motel," Cooper said. "But we ate inside 'cause it was too hot."

"There are several nice shade trees down by the pond, so we can eat outside," Dusty replied and was rewarded by Cooper's hoots of excitement.

They pulled up in front of the dining room door and before Dusty could step out of the cart, Cookie appeared with a medium-size cooler in his hands.

Dusty made the introductions and Cookie gave them his usual taciturn grunt.

"I think he must be a bad cowboy," Cooper said

once the cooler had been loaded and they were on their way toward the pastures and the pond in the distance.

"He's okay, Cooper," Dusty replied. "He feeds all of us who work on the ranch, so in my book that makes him a pretty good cowboy."

"He has bank-robber eyes," Cooper said, obviously not completely convinced. "Look, there's lots of cows!"

They had crested a ridge and in the distance the huge herd of Black Angus cattle grazed on the grass and jostled each other for shade beneath several large trees. Dusty raised a hand and waved to a man on horseback riding among the herd.

"That's Mac McBride. He's our singing cowboy," Dusty said. "On most evenings he pulls out his guitar and plays and sings for us."

"Do you sing?" Trisha asked him.

Dusty shot her a quick grin. "Only in the shower, and only if I'm alone," he replied.

"I can sing. Do you want to hear me sing 'Bingo'?" Cooper asked.

"Maybe later after we fish," Trisha replied smoothly. "Maybe then we can all sing some songs together."

"That would be fun," Cooper replied.

Was this what families did? They fished and ate a picnic dinners, they sang and laughed together? It was all so alien to Dusty. He'd spent every minute of his childhood that he could remember dodging fists and being afraid.

The pond was some distance from where the cattle grazed. It was a nice drink of water stocked with plenty of fish. A wooden dock stretched out about eight feet and made a perfect place to sit and dangle a pole.

"I'm gonna have such fun," Cooper exclaimed as Dusty pulled the cart to a halt.

"We're all going to have fun," Dusty replied.

It took only a few minutes for him to carry the cooler and a navy blue blanket into the shade of a nearby old oak tree. Together he and Trisha spread out the blanket and placed the cooler to one side while Cooper danced around them with an excitement that was contagious.

"And now, the main event," Dusty said and motioned for them to follow him to the edge of the dock where he had fishing poles and foam cups of night crawlers awaiting them.

When he'd been in Bob's Bait Shack earlier he'd picked up two things especially for Cooper. The first was a child's fishing pole and the second was a bright orange life jacket.

"You've gone to so much trouble," Trisha said soberly. "I'll be glad to reimburse you for anything you bought."

"Nonsense," he replied. "It was my pleasure." He picked up the life jacket and then crouched in front of Cooper. "And now, my little buddy, if you want to fish you have to wear this."

"Why?" Cooper held his gaze intently.

"Because only the very best fisherman in the

whole wide world wears this special orange vest," he replied. "Can I put it on you?"

Cooper nodded. Dusty helped him into the vest and fastened it. The last thing he wanted for today was any kind of a tragic accident.

When he stood and looked at Trisha, a burst of warmth that had nothing to do with the sun overhead filled him. She gazed at him with a softness that almost took his breath away.

He cleared his throat and picked up a rod and thrust it into her hands and then handed Cooper his shorter, bright yellow rod complete with a red bobber already on the line.

"How do you feel about worms?" he asked Trisha as he picked up his own rod. "Are you the squeamish type?"

"I've changed dirty diapers. I think I can handle worms," she said with a small laugh.

"Dusty, I don't wear diapers anymore. I'm a big boy." Cooper looked up at him with pride.

"That's good, Cooper. But I could already tell that you're a big boy. And now I think we're ready to hit the dock and catch some fish." Dusty placed a hand on Cooper's shoulder and they all walked out onto the floating wooden structure.

For the next hour and a half Dusty gave lessons to Cooper about how to bait his hook and cast out and then the absolute importance of watching his bobber in the water.

They sat on the dock with Cooper between them and as the little boy focused solely on the task of waiting for a fish to bite, Dusty and Trisha talked about everything from their favorite foods to what crazy things people ordered at the café.

He discovered that she loved Chinese food and that her favorite color was purple. She confessed that she enjoyed watching reality television and was afraid of spiders. Each and every tidbit that he learned about her only made him like her more.

She caught the first fish, a crappie no bigger than his fingers. Cooper wanted to keep it, but Dusty explained that it needed to grow a bit more and the little boy helped him release it back into the water.

"How about we set down our poles for a while and see what Cookie packed for us to eat?" Dusty suggested.

"Sounds good to me," Trisha agreed and began to reel up her line.

"But I want to catch a fish." Cooper's bottom lip began to tremble ominously.

"We'll take a break and eat and then we can fish some more," Dusty said. He was rewarded by Cooper's bright smile.

"Okay, and then I'll catch a fish," he replied happily.

The kid was definitely a little charmer. Trisha took off Cooper's life jacket and when they sat on the blanket, Cooper planted himself nearly in Dusty's lap. It was a strange feeling for Dusty, to feel Cooper's utter trust in him, to know that the boy liked him.

It was equally heartwarming to see the approval in Trisha's eyes. She obviously liked the interaction between him and Cooper.

"Let's see what we have," Dusty said and opened the top of the cooler. "Why don't you help me unpack this thing, Cooper?"

"I can do it. Mommy says I'm a good helper," he said eagerly and began to pull out the containers of food and set them on the blanket in front of them.

As he set them down, Dusty removed the tops to reveal fruit cut up in bite-size chunks, cubes of cheese, ham and cheese sandwiches, and three fat slices of chocolate cake. There was also bottled water and juice.

"Cake!" Cooper exclaimed.

"After a sandwich," Trisha quickly replied.

They ate and talked and laughed and Dusty couldn't remember the last time he'd known such easy joy. Just as Trisha had tackled the worms for bait, she ate with a gusto he found refreshing.

Even with Cooper's presence, Dusty couldn't help the small burn of physical desire she wrought in him. As she slipped a slice of strawberry into her mouth he wanted to chase it with his mouth against hers.

His fingers fought the need to loosen her hair and rake through the silky strands. When she threw her head back to laugh, he wanted to rain kisses down the length of her slender neck. The pearly snaps on her blouse seemed to beg him to pop them open and explore.

Thank goodness Cooper is here to keep you in line, he thought. The last thing he wanted to do was move too fast with her and frighten her away. Still, he couldn't control the hot images that continued to dance in his head.

He also regretted the fact that the day probably

wasn't going to yield any answers as to why she had reacted the way she had the night before to the flowers and note that had been left for her. But this obviously wasn't the time or the place to discuss the topic.

All he knew for certain was that he liked Trisha… he liked her a lot. He admired the way she mothered Cooper and that the three-year-old was obviously secure and happy in his mother's love. That was the way it was supposed to be, that was something Dusty had never known.

He knew she must be a hard worker, otherwise Daisy would have let her go. The brassy red-haired woman was known to be a demanding boss.

She was well liked among the people she served at the café, and he'd never heard a whisper of gossip about her that would send up any red flags in his head.

She was obviously a strong woman. She had no family to depend on and had taken off from her familiar home to build a new life for herself and her son after the tragic death of her boyfriend.

He hoped that this was the beginning of something special between them. And more than anything, he hoped that he could be the man she wanted, the man she could depend on in her life.

The phantom pain shot off in his ear and he fought the impulse to raise his hand to cover it. The only sound he ever heard in that ear was the echo of voices telling him that he would never be good enough for anyone.

If the way to a man's heart is through his stomach, then the way to a single mother's heart is defi-

nitely through her child, Trisha thought as Cooper and Dusty talked about the life of a cowboy.

Dusty had shown infinite patience throughout the afternoon. He hadn't spoken down to Cooper or shown any kind of irritation at the boy with his million questions and abundant energy.

Of course, it didn't hurt that Dusty was definitely a piece of eye candy with his white T-shirt stretched taut across his broad shoulders and emphasizing his slim waist. And she'd never seen a man who wore a pair of faded jeans better than him.

He watched her lips when she spoke, as if he were contemplating another kiss. Far too many times the memory of the kiss they'd shared the night before intruded into her thoughts.

As the two of them snapped lids back on the food containers and returned them to the cooler, Cooper rolled over on his back and within seconds he was sound asleep.

Dusty gazed at Cooper and then grinned at her. "Ah, the action of a true cowboy who has indulged in the three major Fs of life," he said softly.

"The three major Fs," she repeated curiously.

"Fresh air, fishing and food," he replied. With the last of the food put away, he stretched out on his side and propped his elbow up beneath him.

She smiled and mirrored his position on the blanket. "Add in a shortened nap in the afternoon and you get a little sleeping buckaroo."

"He's a great kid, Trisha."

"Thanks. He's definitely the magic in my life," she replied.

"Are all kids his age as bright as he is?"

Trisha laughed. "I don't know about all kids. I only know about Cooper, and I believe he's incredibly smart for his age. I think a lot of it has to do with my babysitter, Juanita."

"Juanita Gomez?" he asked. She nodded and he continued, "Her husband, Richard, worked on the Swanson ranch before he died of a heart attack. He was a good man."

"Juanita has been a real gift to me. She's been babysitting Cooper for the last year and a half, ever since I started working at the café."

"The only kid I've ever spent any time around is Nicolette Kendall's boy when she lived here at the ranch with Cassie."

"Sammy," she replied. "Nicolette, Lucas and Sammy come into the café occasionally. Lucas was one of the cowboys here before he met Nicolette and they moved to the ranch where they live now, right?"

"That's right. Now that they're married, Lucas told me they're starting the legal proceedings so that he can adopt Sammy since his father is dead."

"That's nice. I hope that someday Cooper will have a father figure in his life."

"Lucas was the first of us to find love. Then Nick Coleman wound up falling for Adrienne Bailey and Forest fell for Patience."

"She had a pretty rough time here, didn't she?"

Dusty nodded. "Yeah, her assistant wound up

throwing her in the top of a corn silo in an attempt to kill her. It was a case of professional jealousy at its finest." He shook his head. "Thank God Forest figured out she was in the silo and managed to get her out and in the process the two of them realized how much they loved each other."

She eyed him with open speculation. "Tell me, Dusty, why don't you already have a special woman in your life?" It had been something she'd wondered about for a while. He was handsome and sexy and kind, but she'd never heard any gossip about him and any woman. In fact, she'd never heard any negative gossip about Dusty at all.

His gaze held hers steadily. "I guess part of the reason is that for months I've had a secret crush on you and didn't want to pursue anyone else."

Her heart fluttered and a wave of warmth swept through her at his words. "Then why didn't you ask me out sooner?"

"You don't exactly have a reputation around town for being a dating fiend," he replied dryly. "I know a lot of men have asked you out before and you've turned them all down. It took me forever to get up my nerve and brace myself for what I figured would be an instant rejection. So, why did you agree to go out with me?"

She gazed at her son and then looked back at Dusty. "For the past couple of years my focus has been exclusively on working hard and raising Cooper. It's only been in the last couple of months that I realized I was ready for more in my life." She offered him another smile. "I guess the easy answer is that you were the right man at the right time."

"I'm glad. And speaking of secret crushes, last night you reacted pretty violently to those flowers that somebody left for you." There was an unspoken question in his voice.

The warmth that had suffused her dissipated. She had reacted badly the night before and he deserved some sort of explanation. She also needed to assure him that she wasn't a crazy drama queen.

"When I was younger I had a stalker," she finally replied. "It was one of the most frightening things I've ever experienced. When I saw the flowers and the note, I guess I had a kind of flashback to that time." It certainly wasn't a complete lie, but it wasn't the complete truth, either.

His gaze softened. "I'm sorry you went through something like that, but I want you to promise me something."

"What?" She eyed him cautiously.

"I want you to promise me that if you get another mystery gift, before you freak out and do something impulsive like leave town, you'll call me. I don't want you to be afraid, Trisha, but I also don't want you to go away."

The inner cold that had threatened to grip her never took complete hold as she saw the strength, the sweet possibilities that shone from his eyes. "Okay, it's a deal," she replied.

The blond-haired, blue-eyed man was definitely getting beneath her defenses far more quickly than she could have ever imagined. For the next few minutes the conversation turned to her desire to move out of the motel.

"I'd really like to buy a house, but right now it just isn't feasible," she explained. "I did find two rentals in the paper this morning and I think I'm going to check them out before I go in to work tomorrow. I want to make a move out of that motel room soon."

"I'd be glad to go with you to check them out," he said. "You know, kick the foundation and check out the roof."

"I wouldn't want to take you away from your work here," she replied, although she wouldn't mind having a second pair of eyes to see any potential issues that might arise.

"Our work schedule here is fairly flexible. Cassie doesn't care how many hours we work or when we work them, all she cares about is that the daily chores get done."

"Then I'd love to have you tag along. I'm planning on heading out around eleven. I have to be at work at the café by two."

"Then I'll meet you at the motel at eleven," he replied with an easy smile.

Trisha was slightly surprised by her pleasure at the idea of spending more time with him the next day. Things were definitely moving fast between them, but she wasn't at all sure that she wanted them to slow down.

"Is it time to go fishing again?" Cooper asked as

he popped up from his prone position and rubbed his eyes with the back of his fists.

Dusty laughed and sat up. "Yeah, I think maybe the fish are especially hungry by now."

"Good, 'cause I 'specially want to catch a big fish," Cooper replied.

"Before we go let me hit you with some sunscreen again," Trisha said and pulled a tube of cream out of her purse.

Minutes later Cooper once again wore his life jacket and the three of them were back on the dock with fishing poles in hand. Trisha watched in amusement how Cooper imitated not only Dusty's stance but his facial expressions and actions, as well.

There was definitely a little bit of hero worship going on. Did she worry that Dusty might break her son's heart? Absolutely, but she also wouldn't take this wonderful experience away from Cooper for the world.

As they waited for a bite, Cooper asked a hundred more questions. Did fish have ears? Did they play games in the water? Did Dusty like fish sticks? Did he like fish sticks with ketchup?

Dusty answered each and every question with thoughtful consideration. And then it happened... Cooper's bobber took a dive. He squealed and vibrated with excitement as Dusty hurriedly set down his own pole and helped Cooper reel in his catch.

Cooper whooped and hollered until they had the tiny perch on the dock. "I catched a fish! I catched a fish!"

"You sure did," Dusty replied and crouched down next to the dancing boy.

Cooper grabbed Dusty by the face and kissed him on the cheek. Trisha didn't know who was more surprised, herself or Dusty. He looked up at her with a stunned expression and then quickly gazed back down at the flopping fish on the dock.

"Ah, it's just a baby," Cooper said with disappointment. "It wouldn't even make one fish stick, so I guess we'd better put it back and let it grow bigger."

"I think that's a good idea," Trisha said.

"Now I wanna catch a bigger one," Cooper said once the fish had been returned to the water and his hook was once again baited and ready.

For the next half an hour nobody got any bites and Cooper showed all indications of becoming bored. Trisha had been surprised by how attentive he'd been throughout the day, but now that focus had been lost.

A glance at her wristwatch let her know it was almost seven. She was surprised by how quickly the hours had flown by. She was just about to tell Dusty that it was probably time for them to head back to the motel when he ripped up his pole and his line went taut.

"You got a fish, Dusty?" Cooper asked excitedly.

"I think so." Dusty began to reel in with effort. Trisha couldn't help but notice how his biceps popped with his exertion. Sunlight danced in his hair and she wondered how those golden strands would feel against her fingers.

Get a grip, she told herself even as the memory of

their kiss played provocatively in her head once again. They were still early in their courtship—or whatever they were doing together.

"Is it big, Dusty? Is it a big fish?" Cooper asked.

"I've changed my mind. I don't think it's a fish after all," Dusty said with a frown. "It feels like I'm reeling in a tree branch or a big stick." He continued to reel in a little more easily.

Ripples appeared in the water and suddenly something bobbed to the surface. Smooth and covered with algae, the object shot a wave of horror through her. Was it…was it really…?

"Trisha, take Cooper over to the blanket." Dusty's voice registered a terse alarm.

"But I wanna see the big stick," Cooper protested.

"Come on, son," she said and grabbed him by his shoulder. "You've seen plenty of sticks before." She hurried him away from the dock.

It wasn't until they were seated on the blanket that she fully processed what had been on the end of Dusty's line…a human skull.

Chapter 5

"I'm sorry about the way the day ended," Dusty said two and a half hours later when they were finally in his truck and headed back to the motel. Cooper was sound asleep in his car seat and the deep shadows of night had moved in.

"You don't have to apologize," she replied easily. "I'm sure you didn't plan for this to happen."

He grimaced. No, there was no way in hell he would plan to fish up a human skull from the depths of the pond. The horror of the unexpected catch still rose up in the back of his throat.

"Thank goodness Chief Bowie was already on the property," Trisha said.

Dusty didn't reply. He knew why Dillon had been at the ranch. He'd been conducting more interviews with the men. If the skull turned out to be the one missing from one of the skeletons, it would only make the lawman look more closely at the cowboys on the Holiday ranch. And Dusty couldn't imagine that the skull didn't belong to the skeleton from the burial site.

"I'm just glad Dillon spoke to me away from you and Cooper and removed the…uh…item before Cooper got a glimpse of it," he finally said. "I'd hate to be responsible for him having nightmares." He tightened his grip on the steering wheel, surprised by the surge of protectiveness that rose up inside him as he thought of the little boy.

"I appreciate you calling some of your friends to come down and help distract Cooper."

"No problem." Dusty had called Tony and Mac McBride to the pond to keep Trisha and Cooper company while he'd talked to Dillon and several other officers had combed the area around the pond.

He'd been comforted by the sound of Mac's guitar and Cooper's laughter as they'd sung "Old McDonald" and "Bingo" and other childhood songs.

At least for Cooper it had been a wonderful ending to the day. For Dusty it had been a grim reminder of the murders that remained unsolved, murders that cast a pall over all the men who worked on the ranch.

"Dusty, thank you for everything you did to make today so wonderful," she said as he slowed and turned in to the motel parking lot.

He pulled into the empty parking space next to her car. "It was definitely my pleasure," he replied. He shut off the engine and then unfastened his seat belt as she did the same.

He got out of the truck and hurried to the passenger side, where she had opened the back door to get Cooper. "Let me," he said and gently nudged her aside.

She stepped back and Dusty unfastened the belt that held Cooper and then lifted the sleeping child into his arms. Cooper snuggled against him without awakening. Dusty's heart constricted in an alien but not unpleasant way at the warmth of the little body nestled against him. Cooper's trust, his wonderful innocence, felt like a precious gift.

Dusty carried him to the door, where Trisha pulled out a key and unlocked it, then gestured for Dusty to place Cooper on the king-size bed.

The room smelled of her, of the heady scent of wildflowers and a hint of vanilla. Desire rose up inside him, a desire he quickly tamped down.

She walked back with him to the door and they stepped just outside. "I'll get the car seat out of my truck and put it back into your car," he said.

"Thanks, I appreciate it."

Her eyes glowed silver in the moonlight and beckoned him to repeat the kiss they'd shared the night before. She apparently sensed his intent, for she raised her face and parted her lips as if in anticipation.

He didn't hesitate. He gathered her in his arms and kissed her with all the desire he'd battled through the day unleashed.

She responded in kind, wrapping her arms around his neck and molding her body against his. Her mouth was hot and tasted faintly of the chocolate cake they'd eaten earlier.

The sweet press of her full breasts against his chest, the length of her legs so intimately against his own, created a fiery heat that spread throughout his body. He'd never had such a visceral reaction to any woman before.

He ended the kiss abruptly and stepped back from her, not wanting her to know that he was fully aroused. Her lips were plumped and trembled slightly as she looked up at him.

She raised a hand and touched her lower lip. "You scare me just a little bit, Dusty Crawford."

He shoved his hands in his pockets, afraid if he didn't contain them he'd only reach out for her once again. "I'd never do anything to hurt you, Trisha, although I have to admit, you do stir up my blood."

She dropped her hand to her side. "I have to take things slow, Dusty. It's been a long time since I've had any kind of a relationship with a man. I don't want to jump into anything too fast."

"I don't expect you to. I can be a patient man, Trisha, and I realize we've only just begun to really get to know each other. But I can't promise that I won't kiss you again if the opportunity presents itself."

She laughed softly. "I consider myself duly warned."

He pulled his hands out of his pockets. "So, are we still on for tomorrow?"

"I'd love for you to go with me to look at the rentals," she agreed.

"Then I'll see you here at eleven tomorrow." He

stepped out of the doorway so she could close and lock it.

As he moved the car seat from his truck to the back of her car, he thought of that moment when Cooper had grabbed his face with warm little hands and kissed him on the cheek.

Was Dusty supposed to feel so affectionate toward a child who wasn't his own flesh and blood? He shoved away the question. It didn't really matter how he was *supposed* to feel.

At least Trisha hadn't found any more gifts left at her doorstep tonight. She hadn't told him much about her stalking experience in her past, but Dusty could only guess that a situation like that would frighten any woman.

It was only when he was on the road back to the ranch that the vision of the skull filled his head once again. Talk about a gruesome catch of the day. How many years had that skull been in the pond water only to somehow get dislodged enough that his hook had caught it?

There was little doubt in Dusty's mind that the skull belonged to a skeleton from the burial pit. When he'd reeled it in, he'd seen the jagged wound in the bone, indicating that the person had been hit with a sharp instrument in the back of the head. *Just like the others*, he thought grimly.

Dillon hadn't been willing to make a call about a match until he sent it off to the Oklahoma City lab and got an official match between body and skull, but Dusty had seen the certainty in his eyes, as well.

When Dusty got back to the bunkhouse, Tony was sitting outside his door on a camp chair. "Want a cold one?" He snagged a bottle of beer from a small cooler at his feet.

"Sounds like a plan," Dusty replied. "Just let me get a chair." He opened his door and grabbed a canvas folding chair from his room and then opened it next to Tony's.

"I figured you could use a beer or two after the whopper you pulled out of the pond earlier," Tony said.

Dusty cracked open the bottle Tony handed him and took a long deep swallow of the cold liquid. "I appreciate you and Mac helping me out with Trisha and Cooper. The last thing I wanted was for Cooper to see that skull."

"It was no problem. He's a cute kid."

"Yeah, he is," Dusty agreed. "Have you ever thought about being a father?"

"Never," Tony replied firmly. "I'm not cut out to be anybody's father. What about you? Are you ready to take on that kind of responsibility?"

"I don't know," Dusty replied truthfully. "It isn't something I've given much thought to in the past."

The two men fell into a comfortable silence. Dusty sipped his beer and stared up into the night sky as the events of the day played in his mind.

There was no question that an intense sexual chemistry existed between him and Trisha. But his feelings for her were already so much more than just that. It shocked him how quickly she and her son were worming a path straight into the center of his heart.

Was it simply loneliness that had him feeling this way so quickly? Would he feel the same about any woman he'd decided to ask out? Somehow, he didn't think so. There was just something extra special about Trisha Cahill.

"Have you ever wondered if maybe, just maybe one of us might have killed those boys?" Tony asked.

Dusty turned and looked at him in shocked surprise. The moonlight shone starkly on Tony's high cheekbones and his long black hair. His dark eyes held Dusty's gaze steadily.

"Never…have you?"

Tony broke the eye contact and stared out in the direction of the blue tent that had protected the burial pit where the skeletons had been found. "Just in the past week or so."

He took another drink of his beer, leaned forward and placed the empty bottle in the cooler, and then looked at Dusty once again.

"We both know that the skull you fished up this evening is from the skeleton that was missing a head. I just keep thinking about the fact that somebody murdered those boys and then buried them beneath the loose floorboards of the shed. It had to be somebody who had free access to this property, somebody who knew about those loose floorboards and a deep pond where a skull could be thrown into the water and hopefully never found."

"I can't imagine why the skull wasn't buried with

the rest of the body like the other ones," Dusty replied. It was macabre, to say the very least.

"I guess only the killer knows the answer to that," Tony replied.

"So, do you have a particular suspect in mind?" Dusty asked, even though he didn't want to consider that one of the men he considered his family could possibly be responsible for the murders.

"Definitely not you," Tony replied. "You and Forest were the last boys Francine Rogers brought here. I think the murders had already taken place by that time."

He reached down and grabbed a fresh beer. He cracked it open and then continued, "Brody has always had one hell of a temper, and Jerrod keeps to himself and hasn't ever really shared things about his past like the rest of us have." He released a sigh filled with frustration. "And what about Adam? He was the first to be here, and I don't think he's ever fished in that pond. I don't know, maybe I'm crazy."

"I hope you're crazy," Dusty replied. "All I know is that I never saw any other boys here when me and Forest arrived and I've never heard any of the men talk about any other boys who might have been here before us."

How many of the other men now entertained thoughts like Tony's? Would the suspicion of one another tear apart the brotherhood they had all shared for so long?

Dusty frowned thoughtfully and his heart grew

heavy. Would this be the ultimate end of the family Cass Holiday had so lovingly nurtured?

Trisha dreamed of dead people and skulls and headless skeletons that chased her through the night. She awakened at dawn with her heart pounding rapidly and a scream trapped deep inside her. With a quick glance at Cooper, who still slept soundly beside her, she got out of bed and went into the bathroom.

Thank goodness she hadn't screamed with the horrible visions that had invaded her sleep. The last thing she wanted was to awaken her son with her night terror.

She stood in front of the sink and sluiced cool water on her face and then sat down on the edge of the tub and drew in deep, steadying breaths until her heartbeat finally slowed to a more normal pace.

She occasionally suffered from nightmares, but last night her bad dreams had been even worse than usual. At least Cooper hadn't seen the skull. He hadn't even known that anything bad was happening. Trisha appreciated the way Dusty had handled the situation, not only telling her to get Cooper away from the dock as quickly as he had, but then calling in a couple of his fellow cowboys to entertain her and her son while Dillon and his men dealt with the skull. It had definitely been a ghastly end to a magical day.

As she took a shower she replayed the day in her mind, ending with the kiss they had shared. She had no idea where her relationship with Dusty was going, but there was no question that they shared an intense physical connection.

She'd only experienced that kind of connection one other time in her life, and that had led to horrible consequences that she'd never imagined could happen.

She had told Dusty the truth when she'd said he scared her just a little bit. It wasn't the man who threatened her, but rather the white-hot desire they shared, a desire that could easily cloud good judgment.

Once she was showered and dressed for the day in her jeans and the café's red T-shirt, she left the bathroom and made a half pot of coffee.

Something evil had walked the Holiday ranch. Wasn't that what Juanita had said to her? *It has nothing to do with you*, she told herself. *But could it possibly have something to do with Dusty?*

It was hard to believe that the thoughtful, patient man with his warm smiles and deep dimples could have anything to do with mayhem and murder. But she knew better than anyone that physical attractiveness could hide a cold, black heart and that a warm, charming smile could mask a killing jealous rage.

She only wished now that she had paid more attention to any gossip that had occasionally swirled around the café about the men who worked on that particular ranch.

Proceed with caution, she told herself. That was really all that she could do. She had to be smarter than she'd been in her past. She couldn't let her attraction to Dusty blind her to any negative qualities that he might possess.

Still, she couldn't help the way her heart lifted when he knocked on the door at eleven to go with her to look at the two houses for rent.

"Dusty!" Cooper greeted him with a hug around his waist.

"Hey, little man." Dusty ruffled the mop of Cooper's hair and smiled at both Trisha and Juanita, who had come in early so that Trisha could check out the rental properties.

"You want to play a game with me and Juanita?" Cooper asked and ran back to where Juanita sat at the kitchen table with a game board open in front of her. "It's about candy and it's lots and lots of fun."

"Maybe another time," Dusty replied. "And hello, Juanita, it's nice to see you again."

"And you," the older woman replied with a pleasant smile.

"Remember that I told you that Dusty and I are going to see if we can find a home where we can live," Trisha said to her son.

"And I'll have my own room like a big boy," Cooper said.

"That's right." Trisha walked over and gave him a kiss on the cheek. "Now, you be a good boy for Juanita and I'll see you first thing in the morning when you wake up."

"Why don't I follow you to the café and you can park your car there and ride with me to see the houses?" Dusty suggested once they stepped out of the motel room and into the brilliant sunshine.

"Okay, if you don't mind," she agreed.

His dimples danced with his smile. "Mind? Why would I mind spending every minute of the day that I can with you?"

Oh, yes, the man was definitely dangerous, she thought minutes later as she pulled into the staff parking area in the back of the café.

Clad in a navy blue short-sleeved button-up shirt and his tight jeans, he was as handsome as ever. Even if he grew old and paunchy, he'd still have that incredible smile that warmed her from her head to the tips of her toes.

"All set?" he asked while she got into his truck and fastened her seat belt.

"Ready," she replied.

"Just point me in the right direction."

She gave him the first address, and he pulled out of the café parking lot.

"How are you doing this morning after the debacle of yesterday evening?" he asked.

"All right, although I dreamed about skulls and headless skeletons chasing after me last night," she said truthfully.

He winced. "I'm so sorry."

"Definitely not your fault," she replied. She stared out of the passenger window for a moment. A whisper of uncertainty swept through her as she thought of the crime scene on the ranch.

She turned back to look at him. "I don't think

you've told me yet how you came to work on the Holiday ranch and when you first started working there."

He flashed her a quick glance, and then to her surprise he turned off onto a side street and pulled over to park at the curb. He shut off the engine, unfastened his seat belt and then turned to fully face her.

"Why are you asking me about it now?" His eyes grew darker in hue. "Why do you want to know exactly when I first started working there?"

"I was just curious," she replied.

He stared at her for a long moment. "What's really going on, Trisha? Is this about the skull? Tell me the truth—does this have something to do with the murders?"

A flush warmed her cheeks. She didn't even know how to answer him. "I said I was just curious, that's all," she finally replied.

He looked at her knowingly and then released a deep sigh. "I guess I shouldn't be surprised. I suppose everyone is speculating on which one of us on the Holiday place might be a potential murderer."

"I didn't mean to imply anything," she protested, already regretting the abrupt questions she'd asked.

He stared out of the front window and then turned to face her once again. "I lied to you when I told you that my parents are dead," he said flatly.

He'd lied? Imaginary red flags waved in her head. Why on earth would he lie about such a thing? *You're a hypocrite*, a little voice whispered. *You haven't told him the truth about everything in your life. Just shut up and listen to what he has to say without judging.*

"The truth is I really don't know if my parents are dead or alive. I ran away from home when I was thirteen years old and I never looked back. I didn't want to go into it all this early in our relationship, because I wanted you to know the man I am, not the boy I once was."

"But I want to know everything about you, Dusty." She wanted…needed to know everything about him. Her feelings for him had grown remarkably fast and she had to somehow know if he was just a heartache waiting to happen.

"What did you do after you left home?" she asked, aware that she'd apparently unintentionally opened a can of worms.

"I hit the streets." His eyes were still darker than she'd ever seen them and a knot of tension began to pulse in his jawline. "I probably would have been killed if it wasn't for Forest Stevens. I was a scrawny kid afraid of my own shadow…perfect prey for the bigger, meaner kids on the streets. But Forest took me under his wing, and nobody messed with Forest."

"How on earth did you survive?" she asked. She couldn't imagine Cooper out on the streets at thirteen years old or any other age.

"We slept with one eye open under bridges and in alleys. We stood on street corners and begged for money, and we stole food when we had to." He grimaced. "It's not anything I'm proud of, but we were in survival mode."

Once again he cast his gaze out the front window. "I had just turned fourteen when Francine Rogers, a social worker who worked with the homeless teens, offered the two of us the opportunity to go to a ranch and work for a woman named Cass Holiday. Forest and I jumped at the chance to make something of ourselves. When we arrived there were ten other teens already working for Cass, the same men who have always worked for her."

This time when he looked at her, his eyes simmered with a stark intensity. "I don't know anything about the young men whose skeletons were found in that pit. I never saw anyone on the ranch other than the men I grew up with. Besides, I'm not a killer." He raised his chin defensively to punctuate his words.

She had no real reason to believe him, but she did. Was it her heart overruling her head? Needing him to be the kind of man she wanted? She didn't think so. She had a feeling her doubts about him had been prompted by the skull and the horrifying nightmares that had plagued her sleep.

"Why did you run away from home in the first place?" she asked curiously.

"Because my old man beat me every day of my life and my mother not only allowed it, but encouraged it." The pulse in his jaw ticked faster. "I figured I'd rather die at the hands of strangers on the street than be killed by the people who were supposed to love me."

For a brief moment she saw a flash of a wounded child in the haunted depths of his eyes. "Dusty, I'm so sorry." She couldn't help herself; she reached out and placed her hand on his shoulder.

He shrugged. "It's just a part of my past. Cass taught me a long time ago that I couldn't let it define me."

She pulled her hand back into her lap. "She must have been a good woman."

"She was the very best." He raked a hand through his hair. "Trisha, I have no way to prove to you that I had nothing to do with those murders that happened so long ago. The only defense I have is the truth, and the absolute truth of the matter is that I don't know what happened to those teens." He released a sigh. "I wish to God I did know. Now, do you still want me to take you to see those houses or should I take you back to the café?"

She offered him a small smile and consciously released any doubts that might have momentarily plagued her where he was concerned. "I absolutely want you to take me to see the houses."

"All right, then," he said, sounding relieved. He straightened in his seat, refastened his seat belt and started his truck. As he pulled away from the curb Trisha wondered when—or if—she could ever be completely honest with him about her own past.

Dusty walked around the back of the small two-story house to check out the state of the yard and the air conditioner. Trisha was inside with Damon Wilkins, the owner of the property.

He strode through the dried grass and fought against a wave of odd vulnerability that had risen up inside him at Trisha's questions and the brief visit to his past.

The moment she'd asked him about how he'd come to be on the ranch, he'd known that what she really wanted to know was if he might be responsible for the murders.

Her doubts about him had been the second blow he'd received that day. The first had come at breakfast, when the men had been unusually quiet and the mood somber.

It had been uncharacteristic, and Dusty worried that the suspicions and doubts Tony had voiced the night before had been contagious. Apparently, the discovery of the skull and Dillon's new questions had stirred up a negativity that had never existed before among the cowboys.

He couldn't do anything about it, just like he couldn't do anything if Trisha decided she didn't want to spend any more time with him after this morning. If she really believed he might be the murderer, or even questioned his innocence, then he wouldn't expect her to want to be around him anymore. She was a single mother with a young son and she had to look to her own safety and welfare.

He had absolutely nothing to combat any doubts she might have about him except the truth. And the truth was that he couldn't prove to her in any concrete way that he hadn't murdered those boys.

He shoved away these thoughts and instead focused on the matter at hand. The house's air conditioner was clean and appeared relatively new.

He was far less impressed with the yard. There wasn't a single tree for a boy to climb, and a piece of plywood on the ground covered what looked like an old, dry well. Definitely not a Cooper-friendly environment as far as Dusty was concerned.

He headed back around the side of the house and found Trisha and Damon standing on the small front porch. "I appreciate you taking the time to show us around," she said to the bald-headed older man. "I'll give you a call sometime this evening to let you know what I've decided."

"That will be fine," Damon replied.

She turned and smiled at Dusty. "Ready?"

"Whenever you are," he replied. "I have a feeling that it is a no," he said once they were back in his truck.

She frowned thoughtfully. "It was okay, I suppose. It just didn't scream *forever home* to me. I don't know, maybe I'm expecting too much for the amount of rent I'm able to pay."

"It was a no as far as I'm concerned." He told her about his issues with the backyard. "It just wasn't right for a little boy. Maybe you'll like the second one better."

The next house was an old two-story that needed lots of work inside and out. Peeling paint and a kitchen that Dusty suspected hadn't been updated since the house was originally built made it an instant hell—no as far as he was concerned.

It all shouted of potential headaches, and no matter

what happened between the two of them in the future, that was the last thing he wanted for her and Cooper.

Her discouragement was evident when they were back in his truck and headed toward the café. "Trisha, you've only just started your house hunting. I'm sure you'll eventually find the right one. You just have to be a little patient."

She flashed one of her beautiful smiles. "You're right. I'm just eager to get out of that motel room and into a place Cooper and I can really call home. He deserves something better."

"And you'll find it," he assured her.

"What about you? Do you ever think about owning your own place?"

"I've always considered the Holiday ranch my home, but that doesn't mean if the right circumstances presented themselves I wouldn't make a move." He pulled into a parking space at the back of the café. "There's never really been a reason for me to consider moving out and moving on."

She and Cooper could potentially be his reason, but it was far too soon to tell. He didn't even know what the next few minutes with her might bring after the difficult conversation they'd had earlier.

He opened the windows, shut off the truck engine and then turned to look at her. "I don't know what happens next. I want to see you again, Trisha. I want to spend more time with you and your son, but I understand if you don't want to see me anymore."

"Dusty, why wouldn't I want to see you again?"

"You obviously had some doubts about me," he replied.

Her cheeks flushed a faint pink. "It was the skull and a night of bad dreams. Besides, I can't apologize for being cautious. I like you, Dusty. I like you a lot, and I really don't believe you have a killer bone in your body."

A rush of relief filled him at her words. He hadn't realized until this moment that he'd needed to hear that from her. "For the first thirteen years of my life, I only knew brutality. On the night that I went out my bedroom window, I swore I wouldn't be anything like my father, that I'd be a different, a far better kind of a man."

"Do you like Mexican food?"

He blinked. The question had come completely out of left field. "I love it," he replied. "Why?"

"I make great enchiladas, and I'm thinking maybe we could plan a private dinner for two Wednesday night at the café, since it closes up early that night."

His heart warmed. "You mean to tell me that you not only deliver food to tables and booths, but you also can cook, as well?"

She smiled. "I love to cook, but unfortunately it's difficult to really get into it at the motel with the limited kitchenette and cookware. Let me talk to Daisy and see if it works out, and I'll call you some time tomorrow to finalize the plans."

"I look forward to it," he replied.

Minutes later as he was headed back to the ranch, he felt as if they'd taken a huge step forward. He'd been afraid to tell her about his past, but it hadn't seemed to faze her.

She didn't seem to care that he'd been a kid his parents hadn't cared about except to abuse on a regular basis. Neither of them had even cared enough to go looking for him when he'd finally gotten up the nerve to run away.

Wait until your father gets home.

Just wait until I tell him what a bad boy you are.

He shook the memory of his mother's strident voice out of his head. He'd blamed her even more than his father for the abuse. His father had delivered the actual blows, but his mother had directed the action.

There was no question that part of his attraction to Trisha was the kind of mother she was to Cooper. He knew without question that she would always put her son's welfare above all else, and that's what a good mother should do.

He also believed that he'd helped quell any doubts she might have entertained about him being a murderer. He couldn't fault her for entertaining some doubts, for being careful about who she was inviting into her life. She didn't have just herself to think about, but she also had to worry about her son.

He hoped like hell that Dillon Bowie could solve the crime sooner rather than later. Dusty had a feeling that the longer it lingered, the worse things might get for the men on the ranch.

The afternoon passed as most of them did, with chores that needed to be done before nightfall and then dinner served by Cookie in the cowboy dining room. It was dusk when Dusty got back on his horse, Juniper, to make a final ride through the cattle herd. The night had cooled a little and stars had begun to twinkle overhead.

Would he leave this land to start a new life someplace else? For the first time ever, he knew that he would in a hot minute if it were with his soul mate, his lady love forever.

Happiness and love, it was what Cass would have wanted for all of the boys she'd raised into men. As always, thoughts of the older woman, now gone, created a small well of grief in him. Funny, that he would grieve over a woman who wasn't his flesh and blood but had never grieved over the parents he'd left behind.

As he approached the herd, he spied the silhouette of another cowboy on a horse. Despite the relative darkness, he recognized the other rider as Brody, one of the men Tony had mentioned to him in their intimate conversation the night before.

Even as a sixteen-year-old kid, Brody had certainly been big enough, strong enough to commit the murders. And there was no question that he had a temper.

Dusty tightened his grip on the reins and Juniper protested with a small whinny and a flick of her head. Still, as many years as he'd known Brody, Dusty had never seen him be cruel to an animal or any other human being.

Brody raised a hand to wave at Dusty, and he returned the gesture as he rode the outer perimeter of the herd to check for any signs of a threat from a wild animal.

His gaze cut to the Humes ranch in the distance. It was so much easier to suspect one of the creeps who worked there than any of the men Dusty had grown up with. Many of those men liked fistfights and violence. Although they seemed to share a brotherhood of sorts with each other, they also displayed a lack of morals on many occasions.

Had Zeke Osmond left the flowers for Trisha?

Why would the man care who she was dating if he didn't have some sort of interest in her himself? Or was it some other lonely man in town who had been smitten by the waitress? Trisha was certainly pretty enough to turn any man's head.

It was well after dark when Dusty made his way back to the stables, where he brushed down Juniper and stalled her, and then headed to the bunkhouse in the distance.

Although he was encouraged by how things had gone between him and Trisha, exhaustion weighed heavily on his shoulders. It was more of an emotional exhaustion than a physical one. He was accustomed to the labor required to keep things running smoothly around the ranch.

What he wasn't used to was the brain drain of not just the brief foray into his troubled past, but also the unsettling thoughts about the murders.

No one was outside as he reached his room. It was just as well. He was looking forward to an early night. He opened his door and stepped inside and immediately took off his gun belt and placed it on the top of the chest of drawers. He only wore the gun when he was out on the land and might have to use it against some wild and threatening critter.

He sat on the side of the single bed and reached down to pull his T-shirt off. He paused and frowned as he heard a sound that didn't belong in the room, a sound that immediately shot a burst of adrenaline through him.

Every rancher, every person who had ever spent any time outside in Oklahoma would recognize the dry, papery noise.

Rattlesnake.

Chapter 6

Dusty slowly got to his feet and stepped away from the bed, where the ominous sound came from beneath his rumpled sheets. What in the hell? Adrenaline surged up, instantly vanquishing the deep exhaustion that had gripped him moments before.

Frantically, he looked around and then focused back on the lump beneath the covers. He had nothing in his room to remove a snake from his bed. He also had a healthy respect for ticked-off rattlers, and this one definitely sounded angry and defensive, which made it more than a little bit dangerous.

He banged on the wall that separated his room from Tony's. The last thing he wanted to do was take his eyes off the bed and have the snake slither to someplace else in the room where he might not be able to find it. He thumped again on the wall.

Tony burst through his door with his gun drawn.

"Don't shoot," Dusty exclaimed. "It's just me with a rattlesnake in my bed."

"What?" Tony dropped his gun hand to his side. The man's long black hair that was usually caught into a ponytail at the nape of his neck spilled over his shoulders and he was clad only in a pair of black boxers. He looked at the bed and then at Dusty. "How in the heck did a rattler get into your bed?"

"We can talk about that later after we've removed it."

"We? What's this *we* crap?" Tony replied and laughed uneasily.

"Okay, me. I'll get it out of here. Can you get me a rake?"

"Yeah, right after I get my boots and gloves and maybe a hazmat suit," Tony replied. "You know how I feel about snakes."

"Trust me, I'm not particularly happy about this situation, either. Could you hurry, Tony? I don't want the sucker to move and go someplace else in the room, and I'm definitely not going to sleep with a rattler loose."

"Be right back."

Tony disappeared out the door and Dusty continued to eye the slight bump beneath the sheet. The rattling stopped, but Dusty knew the minute he attempted to mess with it at all the snake would go into defensive mode and that was usually when they struck out.

Tony returned with a garden rake and then stepped back as Dusty held the rake in one hand and used his other hand to slowly pull the sheet from the bed.

He gasped as the sheet fell away to reveal the fairly large, dark brown–banded coiled timber rattler. Its tail vibrated, the rattle sound once again filling the air.

"Jeez, that sucker is huge." Tony remained just inside the doorway, poised as if ready to run for the hills.

Dusty didn't want to kill it, although he wouldn't hesitate if it became absolutely necessary. But a healthy snake population kept the mice and rats around the place to a minimum.

He reached out and placed the flat side of the rake on the snake's back. The snake struck at the metal and Dusty quickly twisted the rake in an effort to get the long body to coil around the implement.

"I'm going to have to grab him with my hand," he said in frustration after several attempts to get the snake onto the rake. He continued to keep enough pressure on the middle of the body to keep the snake pinned into place against the bed.

Carefully he worked his hands down the length of the rake to get closer to the snake's head. "Be careful, man," Tony exclaimed. "You aren't exactly a professional snake charmer."

Dusty ignored Tony and focused all his attention on the writhing creature. A moment of distraction...

a second of carelessness could result in a dangerous venomous bite.

It took three attempts before he finally managed to capture the snake by the back of the head. "You've got him," Tony exclaimed.

Dusty lifted the snake off the bed and Tony raced out the door. Dusty followed and carried the creature away from the bunkhouse and to some thick brush, where he released it. The snake slithered off into the darkness of the night, and he blew out a sigh of relief.

He returned to his room and Tony watched silently as he stripped the sheets from his bed and remade it with clean ones. It was only when the bed was made again that Tony offered to grab a beer for each of them.

"Yeah, I'd say a beer is definitely in order after this," Dusty agreed.

Minutes later the two sat in chairs just outside Dusty's room. "I've got to tell you, I think my heart stopped for a minute when I heard the first rattle," Dusty admitted.

"Give me a pack of hungry wolves or a big old hairy spider any day of the week, but keep the snakes away from me, especially the rattlers." Tony took a drink of his beer and then eyed Dusty. "That snake wasn't some little baby that managed to get in through a crack in the floor. How in the heck did a snake that size get into your room? Into your bed?"

"Beats me." Dusty frowned thoughtfully. "I suppose it probably slithered in during one of the times

I came in or went out of my room through the course of the day."

"A snake that big? And you didn't notice it? Dusty, I know you almost never lock your bunk door. Maybe you should start locking it all the time."

Dusty looked at his friend in surprise. "Man, what are you implying?" Tony remained silent. "Do you really think somebody put that snake in my room?" he asked incredulously.

Tony took another drink of his beer and then leaned forward. "I just think that snake was damned big to have somehow accidentally made its way into your room."

"But why would anyone do something like that?"

"I have no idea. Have you had a problem with any of the other men in the last day or two?"

"No, not at all," Dusty replied. "And I can't believe any of the men here would do something so dangerous."

"All I know for sure is that if you hadn't heard the rattle, then you might have crawled into bed and been bitten who knows how many times before you could get help."

Dusty couldn't help the faint chill of the "what if" that suddenly made the night air feel cooler than it really was. "I just can't believe that somebody would do that. Tomorrow I'll check out my room to see if there are any mouse holes or someplace where it could have found its way inside."

Still, long after he and Tony had parted ways for the night and Dusty was in bed, Tony's words kept playing and replaying in his mind. Was it possible that somebody had sneaked into his room and left him the gift of a venomous snake?

Dusty couldn't begin to imagine who would do such a thing…and why? It just made no sense. There had to be a logical explanation.

The next morning before he set out for chores, he checked the floorboards and walls in the room to see if the answer to the snake's presence was any kind of a hole that might lead to the outside. He found nothing.

He could only assume that somehow the snake had come inside when he'd opened his door and he hadn't noticed it. With the light of dawn it seemed absolutely ridiculous to consider any other possibility.

The morning passed quickly. He skipped lunch with the other men and instead at two thirty he took his lunch break and headed to town and the café.

He could care less what Daisy had for her Tuesday lunch special. It was the woman who delivered it to him that he wanted to see.

He walked in the front door and immediately saw her pouring coffee for local rancher Abe Breckenridge and his wife, Donna. Abe had a fairly successful ranch but he was best known in Bitterroot for the terrific barn dances he threw. Hopefully, if things continued to progress, Dusty and Trisha would be together at Abe's next barn dance.

Dusty walked over to a nearby booth, and his heart warmed as Trisha saw him and her face lit up with obvious pleasure. Oh, he could easily get in over his head with this woman.

"What a nice surprise," she said as she stepped up next to his booth. "I was going to call you later on my break, but it's better to just tell you in person."

"Tell me what?" Dusty asked.

"I spoke to Daisy first thing this morning and we're on for the dinner tomorrow night. The café closes at six, so why don't you come to the back door around seven thirty? That will give me plenty of time to get all of the cooking finished up."

"Sounds great, but are you sure you really want to go to all of the trouble?" he asked.

"I'm positive. In fact, I'm really looking forward to it," she assured him. "Just be sure and bring your appetite."

He grinned. "Trust me, that shouldn't be a problem." He definitely had an appetite all right, but it wasn't for any food she might fix. He was hungry to hold her in his arms once again. He was starving for another kiss with her.

He gave her his lunch order and as she left the booth he leaned back and smiled inwardly. For the first time in his life he truly believed that he was on the right path, a path that would lead to real happiness.

He fought the impulse to knock on wood. It scared him just a little bit. He'd known the contentment of the companionship he shared with the other men. He knew what it was like to enjoy the pride of a job well done. But real happiness was an alien emotion, and deep down in his very soul, he'd never really believed it was possible for him.

Maybe this was all just some setup by fate to kick him in the gut and once again remind him that he'd never be the man he so desperately wanted to be.

At seven fifteen on Wednesday night, Trisha checked the enchiladas in the oven. The sauce bubbled and a layer of cheese was melted all over the top. She turned off the oven, stirred the pot of Spanish rice on the stove and then took off her apron and went into the break room.

When the café had closed at six, Daisy had directed a couple of busboys to move a two-top table into the room. The table was now covered with a pale blue plastic tablecloth and a flameless candle awaited a touch of a button to display its flickering light.

A flutter of nerves shot off in her stomach as she went into the small bathroom to check her reflection. Her cheeks were slightly flushed and she didn't know if it was from the heat of the oven or her anticipation of the night to come.

It's just Dusty. There's no reason to be so nervous. She ran a brush through her hair and then dabbed on some pink lip gloss. She wasn't really nervous in a bad way, but rather in a wonderfully good way.

It was the normal reaction of a woman about to spend an intimate dinner with the man who made her heart sing a little bit louder with every moment they spent together.

She checked her reflection one last time and then left the restroom. She smoothed down the pink blouse she'd changed into after work and turned on the candle and then sat at the table. The food was prepared, the atmosphere was set and all she was missing was the man.

Who would have thought the amiable cowboy who came into the café for a meal once a week or so would have come to mean so much to her so quickly?

The doubts she'd momentarily entertained about him had vanished. Both her head and her heart told her that Dusty couldn't have had anything to do with the murders. He'd told her that he'd been a scrawny thirteen-year-old when he'd run away from home, and he'd only been fourteen when he'd come to the Holiday ranch.

It didn't matter whether he'd been big and strong or puny and weak when he'd arrived on the ranch. There was just no way that she believed he'd had anything to do with the dead boys.

With her momentary doubts silenced, there was nothing left but her growing feelings for him. She certainly wasn't in love with him, at least not yet, but she felt as if they'd been dating for weeks instead of mere days.

As the minutes ticked off to seven thirty, her thoughts ricocheted from Dusty to Cooper. For the past three days Cooper, had talked nonstop about Dusty and the fun he'd had when they had all gone fishing.

Cooper couldn't wait to repeat the experience, but Trisha wasn't sure that she would ever want to fish in that pond again after the skull catch and she would bet that Dusty felt the same way.

There were always other activities the three of them could share together…if tonight went well enough that Dusty wanted to continue to be a part of her life. If, after this private meal with him, she decided she wanted him to remain a part of hers.

She jumped out of her chair at the soft knock on the back door. Another flutter of nerves shot through her as she hurried to let him in.

He wore his jeans paired with a short-sleeved white dress shirt that had narrow navy stripes. He smelled of minty soap, a hint of shaving cream and his wonderful spicy cologne.

"Good evening, ma'am," he said with a formal bow and then thrust a gaily wrapped package into her hands.

"What's this?" she asked and stepped back to allow him through the door. "Dusty, you didn't have to get me anything."

"Flowers seemed way too clichéd to bring to you. You don't have to open it now. It's just a couple of puzzles that I thought you and Cooper would enjoy working together. They each only have sixteen big pieces."

"Thank you, Dusty." A rush of emotion filled her chest. Flowers…candy…even diamonds couldn't have meant more to her. She clutched the package to her heart and then led him into the break room.

"Wow, this is all very nice," he said. His eyes glowed as he looked at her. "You've gone to a lot of trouble."

"Daisy gets some of the credit," she replied and

placed his gift on the nearby shelf next to her purse. "She's the one who arranged for the table back here, although it might have had something to do with not wanting us to sit in the main area where somebody might see us through the windows."

"Whatever the reason, this works for me."

"Then sit down and make yourself comfortable. Before I get our plates, what would you like to drink?"

"Why don't I get the drinks while you get our plates?" he countered.

"Okay," she agreed. "I'll just have ice water."

Together they left the break room and went into the kitchen where only the security lights were on and the main dining area was dark. As she got down two plates, he grabbed a couple of glasses to fill.

"Do you like beef or cheese enchiladas? I made both, along with Spanish rice."

"How about I start with one of each and go from there," he replied.

She dipped up the food and then together they returned to the break room, where they sat at the table across from each other.

The only light in the room was a spill of illumination from the break room bathroom and the dancing candlelight in the center of the table. "This looks terrific, Trisha."

"I hope you like the way it all tastes," she replied.

His gaze lingered on her lips. "Oh, I already know I like the way it tastes."

"You are one wicked man, Dusty Crawford," she said with a small laugh.

He laughed as well, and that set the mood for the evening. As they ate he shared with her more funny stories about the men he worked with and she shared Cooper stories with him.

There was almost nothing sexier than having the same sense of humor as another person. It had been far too long since Trisha had shared laughter with any other man.

The conversation continued to flow effortlessly between them. Dusty cleaned his plate and then went into the kitchen and refilled it, proclaiming that he'd never eaten enchiladas that were so tasty.

"Tell me what else you can cook," he said after he'd finished eating and she'd cleared away their dishes.

"I do a mean fried chicken and homemade mac and cheese. I also love to cook anything Italian or Mexican."

"She's not only incredibly beautiful, but she also fries chicken…definitely a woman after my own heart," he replied with a lazy grin that pooled a well of heat in the pit of her stomach.

"He can not only ride a horse and keep a ranch running smoothly, but he also brings puzzles for me and my son…definitely a man after my heart," she replied.

He leaned back, the amusement gone from his eyes as he stared at her intently. "Too bad there isn't any music. I'd love to hold you in my arms and dance close to you right now."

Her mouth went dry. "Who needs music?"

His eyes blazed hot and he left his chair and moved

around the table to pull her up from hers. "May I have this dance?"

"Absolutely," she replied.

They took two steps away from the table and then he placed his arms around her waist and pulled her tight against him. She wrapped her arms around his neck and released a sigh into the base of his throat as their bodies melded together.

They were supposed to be dancing, but neither of them even pretended to move their feet. Instead they remained perfectly still. She felt as if the only thing that moved at all was her heart, which raced with a rapid beat.

"Trisha," he finally said softly.

She raised her head to look at him and immediately his mouth captured hers. Her fingers curled in the crisp hair at the nape of his neck as she parted her lips.

As he deepened the kiss, everything else fell away. The little table and the rack that held spare café T-shirts disappeared. The table with the plastic cloth vanished. There was nothing but her and Dusty and this moment.

His hands moved slowly from her back to her butt and as he pulled her even closer into him, he gently thrust his hips against hers.

He was aroused, but then so was she. She thrust back, his hardness creating a friction point that shot electricity through her veins.

His hands moved up her back beneath her blouse. Pinpricks of heat fired off everywhere his slightly callused fingertips touched her bare skin. She fought to contain the moan of pleasure that leaped to her lips.

"Trisha," he whispered as his mouth left hers and instead moved down her throat. "You make me half-crazy."

And it was definitely mutual. She wanted to rip off her blouse, shrug off her bra and allow him to touch every inch of her bare flesh. She wanted to tear off his shirt so that their bodies could know each other more intimately.

His lips once again claimed hers and their tongues swirled together in a heady dance that left her weak and gasping. He suddenly dropped his arms and moved back from her.

He raked a hand through his hair and stared at her with an intensity that felt as though he was still touching her physically. "We've got to stop now. I want you, Trisha. I want to make love to you, but not in the back room of the café."

She nodded. He stepped close to her once again, but instead of pulling her back into his arms, he stroked his fingers down the side of her face. "I don't only want the time to be right between us, but I also want the place to be right, and this just isn't right."

"I agree," she replied and drew in a tremulous breath in an effort to slow the rapid beat of her heart. With shaky legs she walked over to the table and picked up her water glass, hoping that the cold liquid would cool her off.

"I don't think a drink of water will help me. What I really need is an hour-long icy shower right about now," he said with a rueful smile. "Maybe it's best if we call it a night. I'll help you put things back in order and then I'll follow you to the motel."

"You know you don't have to do that," she replied.

"And skip out on the chance to give you one last kiss? No way."

Twenty minutes later she was in her car with Dusty's truck right behind her. The night had been a wonderful success and as incredible as it seemed, she realized that she was on the verge of falling in love with the dimpled cowboy.

If somebody had told her that she could feel this way about a man so quickly, she would have denied it was possible. But the heart apparently knew no clock or sense of time.

She parked her car in front of her unit and Dusty was at her door before she could gather her things to get out. She had not only her purse but also an aluminum pan containing the leftover food for Cooper and Juanita to enjoy the next day and the gift that he had brought for her and her son.

"Hand me the food and the puzzles and I'll carry them for you," he said.

She gave him the items and then grabbed her purse and got out of the car. They'd only taken two steps toward her door when she stopped.

No…not again.

Propped against her door was a large box of candy and a white piece of paper. "Trisha, take the food and I'll check it out." Dusty's voice seemed to come from very far away.

Fighting against the familiar frantic fear, she took the container and present from him and watched as he walked to the door and bent down to retrieve the note and the candy.

"Trisha, it's nothing to be afraid of," he said as he returned to her side. "It's just another mystery gift."

"Open the note." Her voice sounded distant and strained even to her own ears.

"YOU'RE MINE."

The words on the paper seemed to scream at her.

You belong to me and nobody else is ever going to have you.

You're mine and I'm all that you'll ever need in your life.

The deep, horrifyingly familiar voice thundered in her brain as she stared down at the note.

"It's just my luck—you get candy and I get a rattlesnake in my bed."

His words penetrated the veil of terror and she stared at him with a new horror. His features were bathed in the motel's neon lights. He looked perfectly calm as his skin turned yellow and then red.

She definitely wasn't calm. "A rattlesnake in your bed?" She stumbled two steps back from him. "When…when did that happen?"

"Monday night."

"Why…why didn't you tell me about it before now?" The fear still torched through her.

He cocked his head to one side. "Why would I tell you about it? It didn't have anything to do with you."

"But it does. I know it does. I have to go… We need to leave town."

He bent down and set the box of candy and the note on the ground. "Trisha, calm down. I told you before that I won't let anything happen to you or to Cooper."

A sharp bark of hysterical laugher escaped her. "I'm not worried about me. He's here, Dusty." Her laughter turned into a choking sob. "He's someplace close and he's already killed. He's going to come after you, Dusty, and he won't stop until you're dead."

Chapter 7

"Trisha, what in the hell are you talking about?" Dusty asked. Her features were so pale in the moonlight she looked like a ghost.

He didn't wait for a reply. Instead he took the container of food and the wrapped gift from her and knocked softly on the motel room door. Juanita answered and he thrust the items at her. "Can you stay for another thirty minutes or so?" he asked.

"Is everything all right?" she asked worriedly.

"Everything is just fine. We thought we were ready to call it an evening, but there are a few things we still need to discuss. We'll be back soon."

"Take your time," Juanita replied.

Whatever was going on, he knew Trisha wouldn't talk about it in the motel room with Cooper present, and he didn't want to stand in the middle of the parking lot to have an important conversation.

What on earth was she talking about? Who in the hell did she think would kill him? All he knew for sure was that he wasn't going to end this night without some concrete answers from her.

He took her by the elbow and led her to his pickup. "Get in," he commanded her as he opened the passenger door.

She moved like a robot and once she was in the truck, he hurried around to the driver's side. He didn't speak as he started the engine and left the motel parking lot with a spray of gravel.

Silently, he drove out of town and didn't stop until they were on a deserted country road. He pulled to the side of the road, killed his engine and then unfastened his seat belt and turned to look at her.

Her face was still unusually pale in the moonlight that filtered in through the truck windows, but her eyes burned with a white-hot fear he couldn't even begin to understand.

"Talk to me, Trisha. Tell me what's happening. Is this about the stalking thing you told me about before? Who is he? Who has you so afraid?" The questions fired out of him.

She blinked rapidly and her eyes misted with tears. "His name is Frank D'Marco and he's Cooper's father." The words seemed to rip from the very depths of her soul.

Cooper's father? What in the hell? "But I thought

you told me that he was dead, that he was killed in a motorcycle accident."

She closed her eyes and wrapped her arms around herself as if fighting off a chill. "I lied, Dusty. I wanted to believe that he was dead." She opened her eyes and looked at him. "But he was never in an accident. Now I think he's here in Bitterroot. *You're mine…* That's what he used to tell me over and over again. He's dangerous, Dusty." Her lips trembled and a tear slipped onto her cheek.

"You said he's killed before. Who?" Dusty's head reeled with this new information, but he wasn't sure how seriously to take any of this. Obviously this was so much bigger than the stalking incident she'd mentioned before.

"I believe he killed my best friend—and my mother." She covered her face with her hands and began to weep in earnest.

Dusty didn't try to stop her tears. He simply reached over and placed a hand on her knee and squeezed in an effort to show his quiet support.

He still didn't have the answers he needed, but he recognized real grief when he saw it and his chest tightened with her obvious pain and heartrending tears.

She cried for several long minutes and then sat up straighter in the seat. She swiped at her face and then dropped her hands to her lap where her fingers twisted together in obvious anxiety.

Dusty moved his hand from her knee and pulled one of her hands into his own. Cold. Her fingers were icy cold as they curled around his. "Start at the beginning and tell me everything," he said gently. "Don't leave anything out. I need to understand everything."

She squeezed his hand as if it were a lifeline in a sea of terror and drew in a deep, shuddery breath. "I was twenty-two years old when I met him at the restaurant he owned with his father and two brothers in Chicago. That's where I lived…in Chicago. He was handsome and charming and we started dating." She shook her head and frowned. "There were so many red flags, but I was young and naive and ultimately so incredibly stupid."

"So, the two of you started dating," he repeated to move the conversation forward.

She nodded. "It quickly got fairly intense. Within three months we were spending most of our free time together and when we weren't together he was either calling or texting me almost nonstop. He was my first serious relationship and I thought all of his attention was sweet, but my best friend, Courtney, worried that he was too possessive and controlling. Courtney didn't like Frank and he didn't like her. Six months after Frank and I started dating Courtney was killed in a drive-by shooting in front of her apartment building." She closed her eyes as if battling against another wave of tears.

Dusty didn't even attempt to process what she was telling him. He needed to hear everything before he could properly assess the entire situation.

She turned her head to stare out the passenger window. "The whole crime was confusing because Courtney didn't live in a high-risk neighborhood where drive-by shootings ever happened. The police also couldn't come up with a motive or a suspect in the crime. As far as I know it's still an open cold case."

"And after that?" Dusty asked softly. He squeezed her hand once again to encourage her to continue.

"And after that Frank was super supportive and our relationship continued. But when he started pressing me to move in with him, I refused. Even though I thought I was in love with him, I liked having my own space. When I got pregnant with Cooper, I still wasn't ready to live with Frank. I just wasn't ready to make that kind of commitment."

She pulled her hand from his and instead worried it through her hair. "The first three months of my pregnancy weren't easy ones. I had terrible morning sickness and my mother came to stay with me. Although Frank didn't say anything, I could tell that he resented her presence. Like Courtney, Mom had serious concerns about Frank. She was even afraid that he was so jealous that he would eventually come to resent the baby and might possibly hurt him. And then when I was eight months pregnant, she was killed in a home invasion burglary. I completely lost it. I was in a total fog until I went into labor with Cooper."

She paused a moment and drew in a deep breath and continued, "Frank was at work and it was as if that first labor pain suddenly cleared my head. I knew in my gut, in the very depths of my soul that Frank had killed both Courtney and my mother and I knew that I had to do whatever I could to get as far away from him as possible."

It was as if a dam had burst inside her and the words couldn't get out of her mouth fast enough. "I packed up all of my personal belongings and everything I'd received as a gift for the baby and then drove myself to the hospital. Cooper was born ten hours later and two days after that, when we were released from the hospital, I got into my car and left Chicago."

Dusty stared at her in amazement. "You couldn't have been healed up from the birth by then."

"I wasn't, but it's amazing what you can do when you're afraid, especially when you're afraid not only for yourself but for your child. I drove for five hours and then checked into a crummy motel where I thought nobody would find me. Cooper and I stayed there two weeks and then I drove some more and checked into another motel…and another."

"What did you do for money? How did you survive?" Dusty's amazement turned to a wealth of admiration as he realized the incredible inner strength she possessed. She'd endured the murders of two people close to her and had run to assure her own survival and that of her son.

"I had some savings that we lived on for the first couple of months and then I finally contacted my mother's lawyer. I knew that I was her sole beneficiary and he had a check ready to mail to me. It wasn't a lot, but Cooper and I lived on that money until I got the job here at the café." Grief once again splashed on her cheeks in the form of new tears.

"And what about Frank? Did you ever hear from him again?"

She shook her head and once again swiped the tears away with one hand. "No, at least not until now." She released a shuddery sigh. "I thought enough time had passed. I thought it was finally safe for me to start to build something normal, but I should have known better."

Defeat shone from her eyes. "You have to take me back now, Dusty. It's time to run. Cooper and I have to leave here."

"No, you don't have to run," he countered. "Trisha, we still don't know if those mystery gifts are from Frank or from somebody else in town. What we need right now is more information. We need to contact Dillon and see what he can find out about Frank. For all we know, the man might be dead or in prison."

"But what about the rattlesnake in your bed?"

"Ah, that critter could have gotten in a dozen different ways. It's not the first time a snake has slithered into one of the bunkhouse rooms," he said dismissively.

Her lips quivered once again. "Dusty, I'm so afraid."

"And we're going to fix that." His brain whirled in an effort to fix things, even if only for the moment. "I don't want you staying at that motel anymore." He turned in his seat, rebuckled his seat belt and started the truck. "We're going to pack your bags tonight and get you and Cooper out of there."

He didn't want her to spend another night where whatever people might be in the other motel rooms were transient. He didn't want her to stay where more gifts could be left for her.

He didn't want her to spend another minute with the fear that shimmered in the depths of her eyes. She needed to feel safe.

"But where are we going to go?" she asked.

"You can stay at the ranch with Cassie." He knew without question that Cassie would take in a mother and a child who needed help. "You'll be safe there. You won't only have me watching over you and Cooper but all the other cowboys on the ranch, as well."

"Are you sure? I mean, I've served Cassie at the café, but we don't really know each other that well." A cautious hope had momentarily stolen the fear that had laced her tone of voice.

"I'm positive it will be fine," he assured her. "We'll get you moved tonight and then we'll talk to Dillon tomorrow. Give it some time before you up and run, Trisha. Let us find some answers that could give you and Cooper a chance—that will give you and me a chance."

"I want that, Dusty, but if I feel like danger is here, if we find out it is Frank, then I'll have no other choice except to leave Bitterroot and find someplace safe."

Once they were back at the motel, Dusty remained in his truck as Trisha went inside and Juanita came out. He rolled down his window as she stopped by the side of his truck.

"I don't know exactly what's happening, but she told me she'll call me when things get settled. I just hope you have their best interest at heart, Dusty Crawford."

"I only want the very best for them," he replied.

Juanita's dark gaze held his for a long moment and then she gave him a curt nod and hurried to her car. Dusty grabbed his cell phone and punched the number that would connect him to his boss.

As he'd assumed, Cassie agreed immediately to him bringing Trisha and Cooper to the ranch house for however long they needed to be there. Cassie might not know yet where she wanted her future to be, but over the past couple of months she'd shown that she had a big heart just like her aunt Cass.

He ended the call and remained in the truck, taking a few minutes to breathe, to think about everything he had learned over the last twenty minutes or so. There was a lot for him to take in.

He was shocked by the story Trisha had told him. Although he had rejected the idea of anyone putting that snake in his room, he wasn't sure what to believe about it now.

Was it really possible that this Frank whoever from her past had found her and was now here in town? Had the man seen them together and put the rattler in his bed in hopes that Dusty would be killed? It sounded so preposterous.

And yet Trisha believed the man had murdered not only her best friend but also her mother because he wanted to be the only person in her life. She thought there was a possibility that Frank had found her and she believed the man would now come after Dusty…

or even more frightening, that he might want to harm Cooper.

Hopefully Dillon would be able to find out something about where Frank was right now. And hopefully he would discover that Frank was in prison or dead or someplace far away from this small Oklahoma town.

Dusty wasn't willing to automatically jump to the conclusion that Frank was here in town. He thought it much more likely that the presents had come from somebody here in town who was harmlessly infatuated. But he couldn't be sure.

He tapped his fingers on the steering wheel and stared at the motel room door. What he really hoped was that he hadn't talked Trisha into staying when there was a clear and present danger to her and her son.

She told Cooper it was an adventure when she awakened him to start the packing process. "Are we going to live with Dusty?" Cooper asked as he shoved his toys into one of the suitcases.

"Not with him, but on the ranch where he lives," she replied. Her heart still raced with anxiety and she had no idea if this new plan was a good one or not. She only knew they needed to escape this motel room, which Frank might be watching at this very moment.

Was it him? His very name in her thoughts caused her heartbeat to increase and the palms of her hands to sweat.

After all this time, had he finally found her? If he

was here, would he kill Dusty to get him out of her life? Or would he try to hurt Cooper in revenge for her ever leaving him? He'd always wanted her all to himself. Once she had gotten away from him, she'd realized that his need for her had been obsessive to the point of insanity.

She had to keep it together. She couldn't let Cooper see the abject terror that still burned so hot inside her. She didn't want any of her fear, any of this madness to touch him in any way.

The task of folding clothes and packing them did nothing to alleviate the sense of impending doom that whispered through her.

She looked up as Dusty opened the door and came inside. His very presence calmed her down just a bit. "I don't know how we managed to accumulate so much stuff," she said, striving for a lightness in tone.

"We got stuff," Cooper said.

"Whatever you can't fit into a suitcase, we'll just wrap it all up in a bedsheet or whatever," he replied.

"Mommy said it's a venture," Cooper said.

"An adventure," Trisha corrected.

"That it is," Dusty replied and started to help Cooper pack up the rest of his things.

It took an hour to finally get everything packed and loaded up. During that time Cooper kept up a steady stream of excited chatter that helped to keep some of her panic at bay.

Finally they were on their way to the Holiday ranch. Trisha had never been afraid of the dark before, but on this night the darkness felt positively ominous. She had only driven about five miles when Cooper fell asleep, leaving her with only her bleak thoughts as company.

She'd never wanted to tell anyone about her past with Frank. She'd not only been embarrassed and ashamed by her own unwillingness to see the danger but had also carried a heavy weight of guilt that she'd been responsible for Courtney's and her mother's deaths.

If only she'd listened to their concerns, if only she'd been strong enough to break away from Frank when she'd seen the first red flags. He'd been so possessive and so focused on her to the exclusion of anything else. It had been sick and unhealthy and she hadn't seen that until it had been too late.

For so long she'd been afraid to let anyone get close to her. The idea of losing anyone else to Frank had been too frightening to bear. She'd finally let her guard down with Dusty.

Certainly he had been nothing but supportive, but why would any man willingly take on this kind of drama? She wouldn't be surprised if in the light of day he pulled back from her, decided that she wasn't the woman he wanted or needed in his life. This thought filled her with a new despair.

She was vaguely aware of the irrationality of her thoughts. She wanted to run. She wanted to stay. She didn't want to put Dusty in danger and yet she worried that he might pull back from her.

By the time they reached the ranch, a different kind of grief pierced through her…if she had to leave or if Dusty decided he wanted nothing more to do with her, then she would never know what might have been with him. She parked her car at the end of the long driveway and Dusty pulled his truck up next to her.

As she got out of the car, the back porch light turned on, and Cassie appeared at the door of the big house. "We'll unload most of the things tomorrow," Dusty said. "I'll just grab the big blue suitcase and the smaller overnight bag and you can get Cooper."

She'd packed the blue suitcase with enough clothes for her and Cooper to last for several days. The overnight bag held all of her toiletries and nightwear.

He grabbed the bags from the backseat and she gathered her sleeping son into her arms. She fought the impulse to squeeze him tight.

Was this the right thing to do? Was she making a mistake in hanging around? She could jump back in her car and just drive away. She could go on the run once again and find another small town in the middle of nowhere to hide in.

Just when she thought the panic would consume her, Cassie approached with a warm, welcoming smile. She placed a hand on Trisha's shoulder. "It's going to be all right, Trisha. You're safe here. Now, come on inside where you can get that sleepy munchkin into a bed."

The panic slowly subsided as Trisha followed the pretty blonde into the two-story house. Dusty walked just behind them with her bags.

They entered into a large country kitchen. Cassie led them through the cheerful room and into a great room, where she pointed to a set of stairs. "At the top of the stairs to the right is a perfect bedroom for Cooper. It has two twin beds. Across the hall is a room with a queen-size bed. Feel free to claim them both for as long as you're here."

"Cassie, I don't know how to thank you…"

"Stop." Cassie held up a hand. "No need to thank me, just go on and get that sweet little boy into bed."

Trisha nodded and headed for the stairs with Dusty just behind her. Cooper didn't stir as she placed him on one of the twin beds. She covered him with a fresh-scented sheet and then went back into the hallway, where Dusty had remained.

"You want me to put your bags in here?" He gestured to the room across the hall.

"No, I'll sleep in here with Cooper." She took the overnight bag from him and placed it on the floor in the room with the twin beds. Dusty did the same with the bigger suitcase.

Together they walked back down the stairs to where Cassie sat on the leather sofa. "It's late for any girl talk tonight," she said and stood. "I just want you to know that you're to make yourself at home and we can chat more in the morning." She turned and smiled at Dusty. "You'll be sure and lock up when you leave?"

"Absolutely," he replied.

"Then I'll just tell you both good-night."

They didn't speak until Cassie had disappeared upstairs, and then Dusty opened his arms to Trisha. She eagerly walked into his embrace. She leaned her head into the crook of his neck and released a tremulous sigh.

It was the first time in hours she felt safe. With his strong arms around her and the comforting scent of his cologne filling her head, she felt utterly protected.

"It seems like it was a lifetime ago that we were eating enchiladas at the café and talking and laughing," she said.

He reached up and gently stroked her hair. "But the important thing is that you're safe now. You don't have to worry about you and Cooper being all alone in the motel room."

"Thank goodness. I didn't want to be there another moment," she replied.

"Tomorrow I'll contact Dillon and we'll see what he can find out. I've got the box of candy and the note in my truck. Maybe he'll be able to pull some fingerprints from them that will let us know who left them for you."

Reluctantly she stepped back from him. "Dusty, I would understand if you don't want to deal with all of this…with me."

His features radiated surprise. "Trisha, I don't want to run from this. I want to help to solve it. I want you free to move on with me."

She searched his face but saw only open honesty and tenderness shining from his eyes. "I want that, Dusty. It's the only thing that's keeping me here right now."

"We both need to get some sleep." He threw an arm over her shoulder and walked her to the back door. A fragile hope built up inside her as he gave her a gentle kiss. "I'll talk to you in the morning."

With this promise, he turned the lock to engage it and then stepped out of the back door and pulled it closed behind him. A moment later the lights on his truck flashed on and she watched until he disappeared from her sight.

The back door also had a dead bolt. She turned it to lock and then left the kitchen. When she reached the top of the stairs, she noticed a closed door at the far end of the hall and assumed it was the master suite where Cassie slept.

Thank goodness for Cassie. It had been an incredibly generous gesture to open her home to Trisha and Cooper without any questions and not knowing Trisha very well.

She went into the bedroom and turned on a small lamp on a stand between the two beds. She was grateful that the dim light didn't wake Cooper, although he always slept deeply. Still, as quietly as possible she opened the overnight bag and retrieved her nightshirt and other items.

Next to the bedroom was a bathroom, and she went there to change clothes and wash her face and brush her teeth. The wonderful highs and the plummeting lows of the night had left her completely exhausted.

All she wanted now was a night of dreamless sleep. She didn't want to think about Frank or her painful past anymore. She didn't want to consider the mysterious notes and gifts that had been left for her.

Hopefully, Dillon would come up with some answers that would put this whole potential disaster to rest. Hopefully, Frank was really in prison…or dead.

She returned to the bedroom and turned off the lamp, but instead of getting into the twin bed next to her son's, she walked over to the window, moved the navy curtains aside and peered out into the darkness.

Once again her heart began to beat too fast and she laid a hand on her chest in an effort to slow it down. Was he here? Was Frank someplace out there right now in the dark…watching her? Waiting for the perfect opportunity to make a move?

And what move would that be? Would he try to get to Cooper? Would he attempt to kill Dusty? Would he try to kidnap her and take her away with him? She couldn't begin to guess what Frank might do after all this time. She only knew that whatever he wanted wouldn't be good for anyone.

She drew in several deep breaths in an effort to calm down. Was she wrong to put her trust in Dusty? Was she once again listening with her heart and not with her head? She didn't want to make another mistake. Were her feelings for Dusty overruling prudent behavior?

With these troubling thoughts, she turned away from the window and got into the small bed. She pulled up the sheet to her chin and waited for sleep to come.

He sat in his car in the alleyway behind the grocery store and drew in deep, gulping breaths in an effort to regain control of his emotions.

He had always prided himself on his rigid control, but tonight he'd definitely lost it. *She'd* made him lose it. He gripped the steering wheel tightly and stared into the darkness outside his window.

Why didn't she understand that she belonged to him, that she would always be his? She would never have a life with another man, especially not a stupid cowboy named Dusty.

His blood began to boil all over again as he thought of the blond-haired man who had ridden off in the night with *his* woman. Sweat began to trickle down the side of his face, a sweat that was anger induced. His chest filled with the force of his rage.

Calm. He needed to calm down. He drew air in through his nose and slowly released it through his mouth. He needed to get his emotions under control in order to plan his next move.

He didn't give a damn about the kid. Cooper—it was a stupid name for the stupid little boy who held a part of her heart. She'd forget about him soon enough.

All he wanted was Trisha. It felt as if he'd wanted her all his life. He rolled down his window, hoping the night air would cool some of the fever inside him. Instead it only filled the car with the nasty odor of garbage from a nearby Dumpster.

He rolled up the window once again and started the car. At least he knew where she was right now. She was at the Holiday ranch. He'd missed the opportunity to take her tonight, but all he needed to do was be patient and bide his time and eventually he'd have her all to himself, the way it was supposed to be.

Chapter 8

"Mommy, I sleeped in my own bed." Two warm little hands landed on Trisha's cheeks. She opened her eyes to see Cooper's beautiful face and the light of a new day drifting in through the window.

"Yes, you did," she replied and struggled to sit up. There had been no nightmares to disturb her sleep, and she felt rested and ready to face whatever the new day might bring. She had to be strong. She had to be tough not just for herself, but also for her son.

"I'm hungry. Do we eat at this new house?" Cooper asked.

Trisha smiled at him. "Yes, honey, we eat here, but only after we've cleaned up and get out of our pajamas and into clothes."

A half an hour later mother and son went down

the stairs, where the scent of freshly brewed coffee eddied in the air. Cassie was in the kitchen seated at the wooden table. She jumped up as they entered the room.

"There you are. I was wondering if I was going to have to eat these chocolate chip pancakes all by myself," she said.

"I like chocolate chip pancakes," Cooper said. "I like them a lot."

"I thought you might. My name is Cassie and I know that your name is Cooper."

"Cooper Cahill," he replied proudly. "And I'm three and a half years old."

"Well, take a seat at the table, three-and-a-half-year-old Cooper Cahill," Cassie replied with a grin.

"What can I do to help?" Trisha asked.

"You can help yourself to the coffee and I'll get the pancakes served right up."

Minutes later the three of them sat at the table with breakfast before them. The meal was accompanied by Cassie answering Cooper's million questions about the ranch and Dusty.

"I like Dusty a whole bunch," he said with a dollop of syrup decorating his chin. Trisha leaned over and wiped the goo off with her napkin.

"I like him, too," Cassie replied. "I like all the cowboys who work here."

"Mac and Tony sang songs with me and Mommy. Do you know how to sing 'Bingo'?"

"Honey, we don't sing at the table," Trisha said before Cooper could show off his rowdy pipes.

"Maybe later you and I can sing together," Cassie said, earning her a smile of approval from Cooper.

"Dusty brought in another suitcase earlier," Cassie said when Cooper had cleaned his plate. "He mentioned that it was filled with Cooper's toys. I think there's also a gift that he said you could open if it was okay with your mom. It's all in the great room waiting for you to unpack it."

"A gift? But it's not even my birthday," Cooper said. He looked at Trisha eagerly.

"Go ahead and open it," she said. "You can play with your toys and the gift, but don't touch anything that doesn't belong to you," she added.

"I won't," he said as he scooted out of his chair.

"What a cute kid," Cassie said once he'd left the room.

"Thanks." Trisha wrapped her fingers around her coffee cup.

"Dusty also brought in the leftover enchiladas you made. He told me he put them in the bunkhouse refrigerator overnight so that they wouldn't go bad."

Trisha nodded. "I'm not sure what all Dusty has told you…"

"He told me enough for me to know that you and Cooper are exactly where you need to be for as long as you need to be here."

"Hopefully it's just for a couple of days or so. I'll be more than happy to pay you something for rent," Trisha said.

"Don't be silly. The truth is I'm going to enjoy having you two here. This house gets pretty lonesome with me being here all by myself. Nicolette and her son, Sammy, came here with me from New York City. Since they moved out, I've missed having a young one around. We're all going to get along wonderfully, Trisha."

Her words, along with the warmth of her smile, assured Trisha of their genuine welcome. They had just cleaned up the dishes when Dusty appeared at the back door.

"Good morning," he said as he stepped into the kitchen. As always he looked hot in his faded jeans and a navy blue T-shirt.

"Dusty!" Cooper came running back into the room. He launched himself into Dusty's arms. "You got me puzzles and it isn't even my birthday!"

Dusty laughed and set Cooper back down on the floor. "Those are for you and your mother to put together."

"What do you say to Dusty, Cooper?" Trisha asked.

"Thank you, thank you and thank you! Now I gotta go, the bad cowboys are tearing up the town." They all laughed as he disappeared back into the great room.

The laughter in Dusty's eyes faded as he gazed at Trisha. "I just wanted to let you know that I've already spoken to Dillon this morning. He's going to meet you here around eleven to discuss your…uh, issue. If you don't mind, I'd like to be here with you when he arrives."

"I'd like that," she replied.

"And I'll be glad to occupy Cooper while you talk to Dillon," Cassie said.

Trisha looked at her gratefully. "Thanks. This isn't something I want to discuss in front of him. He's too young for these kinds of adult things."

"Then I'll just get out of here and I'll be back around eleven," Dusty said.

"He's a good man," Cassie said when he was gone.

"I'm finding that out with every minute I spend with him," Trisha replied. "I just hate that he's been pulled into my drama."

Cassie smiled. "Trisha, if he didn't want to be in your drama, then he wouldn't be. One thing I've learned in the relatively short time I've been here on the ranch is that the men who work here are not only great workers, but they're also headstrong and know what they want when they want it. You could definitely do a lot worse than Dusty."

"I already have," Trisha replied darkly, a sliver of fear edging through her as she thought about what Dillon might find out about Frank's whereabouts.

"I think there's a child gate in one of the storage buildings," Cassie said as they cleaned up the dishes. "I seem to remember seeing one, although I have no idea why Aunt Cass would have had it. I'll have Adam see if he can locate it and bring it inside. I'd feel better if we put it up at the top of the stairs."

A new wave of gratitude swept through Trisha. She'd already worried a bit about the stairs and Cooper getting disoriented in the middle of the night or in the morning and leaving the room without awakening her. "That would definitely put my mind at ease. If he can't find it, then I'll pick one up in town. Speaking of town, I need to call Daisy and let her know I won't be coming in to work for at least a couple of days."

"Go make your call, I'll finish up in here," Cassie replied.

At least Daisy didn't ask questions. She simply told Trisha to take as much time off as she needed and to let her know when she was ready to return to work.

Trisha didn't know when or even if she would be ready to return to work. Her future was on hold here in Bitterroot. No matter how much she had grown to care about Dusty, her fear of Frank was much bigger.

He was the monster in the closet and the boogeyman under the bed. She knew what he was capable of, and the last thing she wanted was for Cooper or Dusty to come to any harm just because they were important in her life. She'd run long before she'd ever let that happen.

The morning crept by as she anticipated meeting with the chief of police. She didn't know Dillon Bowie well, but he'd always been kind to her when he'd eaten at the café.

Adam arrived with the child gate at ten thirty and installed it at the top of the stairs and then left to head back outside.

"Hey, Cooper, how would you like to learn how to paint a picture?" Cassie asked when Adam was gone and it was almost time for Dillon to arrive.

"Can I paint a cowboy?" he asked.

"You can paint whatever you want," she replied

with a quick glance at Trisha. "I've got all my paints and canvases up in my bedroom. We'll go up there to paint some pictures."

Cooper looked at Trisha for permission. "Go have fun with Cassie," she said and then gave the woman a grateful look. "When you're finished, we'll frame it and hang it in our new home."

"Cool," Cooper exclaimed.

Cassie took him by the hand and led him up the stairs at the same time that Dusty came in through the back door. "How are you doing? Are you ready for this?" he asked with a concerned look on his face.

"I guess I'm as ready as I'll ever be." She motioned him to a chair at the table and sank down across from him. "I can't believe how nice Cassie is being to us."

"There are lots of good people in Bitterroot and she just happens to be one of them," he replied.

"That's what I've loved about living here—there are so many wonderful people. I was hoping to make this a home for us forever." Would that ever happen now or would she have to pick up and start all over again? How many times in their lives would they have to move to keep escaping Frank? The thought was definitely depressing.

"That can still happen, Trisha. Even if it is Frank, maybe it's time you stop and take a stand against him. Maybe it's time you fight for what you really want."

The very idea shot a burst of Arctic wind through her. "How do you make a stand against a monster?" She shook her head and leaned back in the chair.

"You stand side by side with the people who care

about you," Dusty replied. "You aren't alone this time, Trisha. You have people to stand with you... you have me."

Anything else he might have said was halted by a knock on the back door. Dusty got up to answer and returned with Chief of Police Dillon Bowie.

Dillon's handsome features were pulled taut and tension radiated out from his gray eyes. "Trisha," he greeted her as he sat in the chair opposite her at the table and Dusty moved to sit next to her.

"Good morning, Dillon. I'm sorry to have to add to your troubles by calling you out here," she replied.

"I've already had a morning of trouble, and I would have had come to talk to you in any case," he replied.

"Why? What happened this morning?" Dusty asked with slightly narrowed eyes.

"I got a call from Fred Ferguson this morning asking me to come out to the motel. He said some vandalism occurred overnight," Dillon explained.

A new case of nerves began to jangle inside Trisha as she exchanged a quick glance with Dusty. "Vandalism?"

Dillon nodded and pulled a notepad and pen from his pocket. When he looked at Trisha again, his eyes held a wealth of speculation. "I'm assuming you and Dusty didn't trash your room when you left the motel last night."

"Of course not," she replied, the nervous electricity in her veins sizzling even hotter.

"Somebody did," Dillon said curtly. "The front window was broken out and the bed was slashed to ribbons. The microwave was smashed on the floor, along with everything else that wasn't bolted down. A huge rage exploded in that room."

Trisha stared at him in horror. Somebody had broken into the motel room? How soon after she and Dusty had left? If they had taken fifteen more minutes to finish up the packing, would they have been confronted by somebody who had a killing rage? And what if Dusty hadn't arranged for her to leave? What if she'd been in that room alone with Cooper?

Had Frank decided to make a bold move? Had he believed that Trisha and Cooper were in the room? Or had it been somebody else…somebody she wouldn't see coming because she didn't know who he was?

Dusty listened intently as Trisha told Dillon what she'd shared with him the night before about the man who was Cooper's father. Once again a simmering panic radiated from Trisha's eyes, put there in part by the news about the motel room.

Had somebody watched them last night while they'd packed up her things and left? Or had that somebody come to the room to present himself to her and when he realized she was gone he went totally nuts?

No matter the scenario, Dusty didn't like it. He didn't like it one bit. This was different than some innocent secret admirer.

"Did you tell the police of your suspicions concerning Frank at the time?" Dillon asked.

"I called the detective in charge of my mother's

murder case on my way out of Chicago. He told me they were investigating the crime, but I never heard anything else from him," Trisha replied.

"And the detective's name?"

She frowned. "Eric Kincaid."

Dillon wrote down the name and then leaned back in his chair. "Now, Dusty mentioned that some things were left at your motel room on a couple of occasions. Tell me about it."

She told him about the flowers, the candy and the two notes that had been left for her. Once again her voice trembled with barely suppressed fear.

"I've got the box of candy and the note that was left for her last night in my truck," Dusty said when she'd finished.

"I'll get them from you as I leave." He turned his attention back to Trisha. "Do you have any idea who in town might have left those things for you?"

"I don't have a clue," she replied. She placed her hands on the tabletop and twisted her fingers together.

"A pretty woman like you surely gets a lot of male attention. Is there some man who has been especially friendly lately? Maybe somebody who asked you out and you rejected them?"

"There have been a few in the past," she replied. "But nobody who really stands out in my mind. I mean, I have some regular customers who always sit in my section when I'm working and they're all friendly to me."

"Give me some names," Dillon said.

Trisha frowned once again. "I don't want to cause

trouble for anyone who isn't responsible for all of this."

"Trisha." Dusty reached over and covered her hands with one of his. "If we want to get to the bottom of this, then you need to tell Dillon what he needs to know to start an investigation."

"Besides, I'm not going to run out of here and arrest everyone you tell me about," Dillon said wryly. "In any case, it isn't a crime to leave gifts anonymously. But what happened in that motel room last night is definitely a crime, and I want whoever is responsible for that."

Trisha's frown deepened. "Steve Kaufman is a regular of mine. He just sits and mostly reads, but I've sensed that he might be a little interested in me."

Dusty pulled his hand back from hers and leaned back in his chair as she continued to name men. He was vaguely surprised by who all had asked her out in the past and more than a little bit curious if one of them was her secret admirer.

It was too bad that nobody at the motel had witnessed who had wreaked havoc in unit 4. Unfortunately, Dillon had told them, the units on either side of hers had been empty last night.

"You might want to check out Zeke Osmond," Dusty said when she'd finished with her list of names. He told Dillon about his brief conversation with Zeke at the café the day after he and Trisha had gone to the Watering Hole.

Dillon sighed. "Why is it that whenever there's trouble, Zeke's name always manages to come up?"

He shook his head and looked at Trisha once again. "Anyone else you can think of?"

"Several of the men from the Humes ranch usually sit in my section whenever I'm working, but Zeke is the only one who ever asked me for a date. None of the rest of them ever asked me out, although they are sometimes suggestive, bordering on lewd," she replied.

"When did Zeke ask you out?" Dusty was surprised at this bit of news.

"Maybe six months ago." She frowned. "It was just kind of off-the-cuff and I told him that I didn't date." She looked at Dillon once again. "How long will it take for you to let me know something about Frank?"

Dillon shrugged and stuck his pad and pen back into his shirt pocket. "I'll make some phone calls when I get back to the station and see if I can hook up with Detective Kincaid. I'll let you know as soon as I know something." He stood and looked at Dusty. "If you walk out with me, I'll take those items you have in your truck."

"I'll be right back," Dusty said to Trisha as he and Dillon got up from the table.

The two men left by the back door and headed in the direction of the shed where Dusty's truck was parked. "So, what do you think?" Dusty asked.

"To be honest, I don't know what to think," Dillon replied. "It's obvious she believes that this Frank character is not only here in town but also presents a real threat to her and her son. If he's really the monster she thinks he is, then it's hard to believe a character like that would leave any gifts for her that would warn her of his presence here."

"It's equally hard to believe that somebody here in town would harbor the kind of rage that was apparent in that motel room," Dusty said darkly.

They walked a few minutes in silence. "When is that coming down?" Dusty asked as they moved past the blue tent.

"I was going to have a couple of men come out later this afternoon and take it down. I'm sure Cassie will be glad to have it finally off the property."

"We all will be glad," Dusty replied. "Anything new on the case?"

"Nothing. I'm still waiting to hear from the lab about your fishing prize."

"You know it's going to be a match to the skeleton that was missing a skull."

Dillon released a deep sigh. "Yeah, I know. In the meantime, I hope I can give Trisha some answers sooner rather than later. I'd like to get to the bottom of her issue so that I can get back to trying to figure out who is responsible for those skeletons."

"Right now all I care about is Trisha and Cooper," Dusty replied.

By that time they'd reached the shed. Dusty led Dillon to his truck and opened the passenger door. He stared at the seat where the box of candy and the note had been.

They were gone.

He turned to look at Dillon. "I had them right here last night." He bent down to check the foot area. Nothing. "They're gone. Somebody must have come in here and taken them."

"Crap," the lawman said eloquently.

Dusty mentally echoed the sentiment. Who had gotten into the shed? Was it possible that Trisha's secret admirer was one of the men who worked on this ranch, somebody whom Dusty considered a brother?

Dusty didn't tell Trisha about the missing items when he returned to the house. Cooper and Cassie had come back downstairs, and Cooper greeted him with excitement. "I painted a picture," he declared proudly.

"You did? A picture of what?" Dusty asked.

"It's you on a horse. Cassie helped."

Never in his life would Dusty have imagined the warmth of pleasure that worked through him at the idea of a three-year-old painting a picture of him. "That's terrific, Cooper. When can I see this work of art?"

"It's drying right now," Cassie said. "We thought we'd have a little art show after dinner tonight."

"An art show and ice cream, right, Cassie?" Cooper said.

She smiled at him with obvious affection. "That's what I promised." She looked at Dusty. "Maybe you can come back up here around seven?"

"Sure," Dusty agreed. "And now I'd better get to work." He looked at Trisha. "Walk me out?"

"Cooper, while your mom goes outside with Dusty for a minute, why don't you and I figure out what we're going to eat for lunch," Cassie said.

As Dusty and Trisha stepped out the back door,

Cassie and Cooper opened the refrigerator door and discussed the merits of grilled cheese.

The minute they were alone on the back stoop, Dusty fought the impulse to draw Trisha into his arms. Her face was pale and her eyes were dark from the toll of the conversation with Dillon.

"I know all of this has been very stressful for you," he said instead.

"Stressful, but I also feel oddly relieved in telling Dillon everything. Frank has been a secret for too long and now he isn't anymore."

"Dillon is a good man, Trisha. He's a smart man. Right now all we can do is trust that he'll figure all this out."

"It's been a long time since I put my trust in anyone."

"I hope you know that you can trust me," he replied.

She gazed at him for a long moment, and some of the darkness in her eyes lightened. "I do trust you."

He smiled at her with forced optimism. "We're going to get through this, Trisha."

"I desperately want to believe that. And now I'd better get back inside before Cooper convinces Cassie to have cake and cookies for lunch." The tension that had tightened her features relaxed a little. "I guess I'll see you this evening for ice cream and an art show."

"I wouldn't miss it."

He waited until she'd disappeared into the house before turning to head back to the stables, where today he was in charge of cleaning and oiling tack.

As he walked, his thoughts returned to the missing candy box and note. Cooper's suitcase of toys and the puzzles had been in the back of his pickup. When he'd grabbed them earlier that morning, he hadn't thought about checking on the candy and the note in the passenger seat in the cab.

How in the hell had anyone known they were in his truck? Was somebody watching his every movement? Trisha's?

His gaze shot to the Humes ranch in the distance. She'd named four men who worked on the neighboring ranch and usually sought out her section to eat in when they came into the café.

Zeke Osmond was a known creep, as was the older Lloyd Green. Greg Albertson and Shep Harmon had never given Dusty much trouble, but that didn't mean anything.

Was one of them responsible for everything that was happening? Certainly their proximity made them jump to the top of any list of suspects.

Any one of them could have crept across the property in the darkness of night and gotten into his truck. With a set of binoculars, one of them could have watched Dusty and Trisha pull into the driveway the night before. It was certainly easier to believe that possibility than embrace the idea of one of the men here being responsible for anything negative.

He entered the stables and went directly to the tack room. He sat down on a bench but didn't immediately begin his work. His thoughts continued to tumble over themselves in his head.

Rage.

That was what Dillon had described he'd seen in the destroyed motel room.

Rage.

Was it Frank? Or was it possible that someone's secret crush on Trisha had transformed into that intense negative emotion? Was it a case of a crazy obsession turned bad?

Had Zeke harbored a secret resentment toward Trisha that had simmered for six months since she'd turned him down for a date? Had that resentment flared into something worse when he'd realized that Trisha was dating Dusty? It was impossible to know for sure.

Somebody had to have known that those things had been in his truck—somebody who now surely knew that Trisha and Cooper were here on the ranch.

Dusty wanted to protect her and Cooper against any harm, but how did he fight an unknown entity? How could he guess from where danger might come?

Are you really strong enough?

Are you really smart enough?

The resounding self-doubts echoed in his brain. He shook his head in an attempt to dispel them. *You aren't that sniveling punk anymore*, he reminded himself.

Are you really strong enough?

He only hoped that when push came to shove, he was capable of doing whatever was necessary to keep Cooper and Trisha safe from harm.

Chapter 9

"It's nice to finally have that blue tent gone," Cassie said late that evening after the art and ice cream party had come to an end and Dusty had left to return to the bunkhouse. Cooper was in bed and the two women lingered in the kitchen over glasses of iced tea.

"I can't imagine how horrified you must have been when those skeletons were first found," Trisha said and fought off a shiver that threatened to walk up her spine. It seemed as though her thoughts kept going to all things bad…skeletons, stalkers and things that went bump in the night.

"It was definitely more than a little sobering." Cassie paused to take a drink. When she placed her glass back on the table, a frown furrowed her brow. "It was crazy to find out that I'd been left this ranch by an aunt I hardly knew, but definitely horrifying to realize I'd also inherited a decade-old murder mystery, as well."

She cast her gaze out the window, where the darkness of night was profound, and when she turned back to look at Trisha she gave her a wry smile. "You have a crazy ex-boyfriend in your past and lately I've been wondering if maybe my aunt Cass might have had a little bad crazy in her."

Trisha looked at her in surprise. "Dusty thinks Cass hung the moon."

"Yeah, so do all of the other cowboys here, but they'll also tell you she was tough as nails. Rumor has it that she could flick a cigarette out of somebody's mouth with her bullwhip and she took no guff from anyone."

"Do you think she might have had something to do with the murders?" Trisha asked.

Cassie swept a hand through her blond hair and released a sigh. "To be honest, I don't know what to think. I found a bunch of her diaries in an old shed and I've been slowly working my way through them to learn more about her and her life. Unfortunately, by the time I go to bed to do a little reading, I end up falling asleep. These ranch hours are definitely different than the ones I kept when I was in New York."

"I heard you had a shop there. That must be exciting."

Cassie laughed. "I suppose it's exciting if you like stress. The truth is I've spoken with the landlord, who is a friend of mine, and at the end of the month he's going to pack up the contents of the store and put them in storage for me."

"Does that mean you've decided that you're going to stay here in Bitterroot?"

Cassie frowned once again. "To be honest, I don't know what the future holds for me. I haven't made up my mind yet whether I want to stay here or go back to New York. My heart is really still in the city and with my art, but there are things that need to be taken care of around the ranch before I'd put it on the market."

"I'm sure everyone here wants you to stay," Trisha said.

Cassie nodded. "Some of the men have been quite vocal about wanting me to stay and not sell out." She leaned back in her chair. "You and Dusty seem to have a good thing going on."

Trisha's cheeks warmed. "He's something special. What about you? Have you met any cowboy who makes your heart beat a little faster?"

"I don't want to meet anyone who might make my decision about leaving here more difficult."

Trisha smiled. "It's funny—you aren't sure if you want to stay here, and I don't want to leave."

"Maybe you'll hear something from Dillon tomorrow that will set your mind at ease."

"I hope so, and now I'd better get up to bed. That little man of mine will be up early." Trisha finished the last of her iced tea and then put her glass in the dishwasher.

A half an hour later she was in the twin bed. She

stared up at the darkened ceiling and listened to Cooper's soft sleeping breaths.

She couldn't help thinking once again of the trashed motel room and what it implied. She'd called Fred Ferguson, the owner of the motel, earlier in the day to tell him how sorry she was about the room.

Fred had assured her that he didn't hold her responsible and he was as eager as anyone for Dillon to come up with the guilty party.

She'd hoped that Dillon would have some news for her before the end of the day. *Hopefully he'll have news for me tomorrow*, she thought as she drifted off to sleep.

The next day passed agonizingly slowly as she waited for a phone call or a visit from the chief of police. Cassie left just before noon with her foreman, Adam, to deal with some ranch business, and Trisha and Cooper ate lunch and then he went down for a nap.

While he slept, Trisha paced the great room and finally settled on the sofa and turned on the television, but the game show couldn't hold her attention.

As nice as Cassie was, Trisha and Cooper couldn't stay here forever. Trisha also couldn't go weeks without getting back to work. Maybe it would be best for everyone if she and Cooper really did leave town.

A small voice in her head cried out as she contemplated leaving Dusty. He already had more than a piece of her heart. She could see a future with him. She could visualize a life with him. But at what cost?

Thankfully, Cooper woke up and Cassie returned

home. Their cheerful chatter managed to pull Trisha out of her black thoughts…at least for the moment.

It was just after dinner that Dusty came to the back door. "I thought maybe you and Cooper might like to come outside and play," he said with his charming smile.

"What are we gonna play, Dusty?" Cooper asked eagerly.

"I thought you could bring your cowboy figures outside and your mom and I can watch while you build a town."

"Cool!" Cooper replied. "Can we?" He turned to Trisha with excitement. "Can we play outside?"

"Sure, that sounds like fun," she agreed.

"There's a couple of lawn chairs in the garden shed," Cassie said.

"Thanks, I already grabbed them," Dusty replied.

Twenty minutes later Cooper was busy making buildings from sticks and rocks that Dusty had gathered as Trisha and Dusty watched from the comfort of the chairs.

"Good day?" Dusty asked. He looked at her as if he wanted to see each and every thought she'd had while he was absent.

"It was a long day. I was hoping to hear something from Dillon," she replied.

"I'm sure he'll let you know just as soon as he knows something," Dusty replied. "The crimes that you think Frank committed didn't just happen yesterday," he reminded her softly.

"I know, but I can't stay here with Cassie forever,

and sooner rather than later I need to get back to work."

"Trisha, it's only been two nights." His gaze held hers intently and then a smile curved his lips. "Don't make me hog-tie you to keep you here."

She couldn't help the laughter that bubbled out of her. "You and what army, cowboy?"

The amusement in his eyes faded. "I'm serious, Trisha. Give this a chance."

"I'm not going anywhere," she replied. *Yet.* She wasn't going anywhere yet, but she couldn't help the anxiety that was a living, breathing entity inside her.

For the next hour they watched Cooper play and Dusty talked about everything he had done during the day. The tension that had knotted in her stomach throughout the day slowly began to unwind as she listened to him talking about oiling tack and riding and cleaning out stalls in the stable.

When she was with Dusty, all things seemed possible. The world was a less frightening place when he smiled at her. Gazing into the clear blue of his eyes made her believe that maybe...just maybe real happiness could finally be hers.

As the evening deepened, cicadas sang in the trees and Trisha couldn't help but think how wonderful it would be if she could spend every night like this... sitting with Dusty as they watched Cooper play.

"This is nice," she said.

"I was just thinking the same thing," he replied with an easy smile.

"Look, Dusty, this is the jail for the bad guys," Cooper said and pointed to a rock structure.

"That looks like a great jail," Dusty replied.

"The good cowboys got all the bad guys and they can't get out of this jail," Cooper replied.

Trisha was just about to call it a night so she could get Cooper into a much-needed bath before bedtime when the sound of a car coming down the long drive froze her in her chair.

Dillon's patrol car came into view and he pulled to a halt at the end of the driveway. Instantly, the knot of tension returned to the pit of her stomach.

Dillon got out of his car and walked toward them. The grim set of his features did nothing to alleviate Trisha's stress. Before he could greet them, Cassie stepped out of the back door.

"Evening, Dillon," she said.

Despite her nerves, Trisha thought she heard a new lilt in Cassie's voice.

"Cassie," he returned as a small smile danced on his lips. The smile disappeared as he greeted Trisha and Dusty.

"Hey, Cooper, why don't we go inside," Cassie said. "I think I'm hungry for some cookies and milk before bedtime."

"Me, too," Cooper agreed eagerly. "I like cookies and milk even if it isn't bedtime."

"Then let's go," Cassie replied.

"Sorry it's taken me this long to get back to you," Dillon said once Cassie and Cooper had disappeared into the house. "I only just managed to connect with Detective Kincaid about an hour ago."

"And?" Trisha leaned forward, her heart thrumming a quickened beat. She felt as if her entire life hung in the balance, waiting for Dillon to speak.

"And he told me that both your mother's and Courtney's murder cases remain unsolved. Frank D'Marco was their number-one suspect at the time, but they couldn't pull together any evidence to arrest and charge him."

"Does he know where D'Marco is now?" Dusty asked. He also leaned forward in his chair.

"According to Kincaid he's been off the grid," Dillon replied.

Trisha frowned. "Off the grid? What exactly does that mean?"

"Six months after you left Chicago, he disappeared. Since that time there have been no earnings assigned to him, no vehicle registered to him and no address or phone number. I also did some checking and I know he isn't dead or in prison."

"So, it's possible he's here in Bitterroot," Trisha said faintly.

Dillon's features tightened. "Yes, I guess it's possible."

Trisha drew a deep breath and stared past Dillon to a stand of trees in the distance as her heartbeat quickened and fear screamed silently in her head.

"Trisha, we really don't know any more now than we did before Dillon arrived," Dusty said once the lawman had left. "It's possible he's here, but it's also possible he isn't. Dillon now has a picture of the man and he told you he's distributed it to all of his officers. If this creep is here in Bitterroot, then somebody will see him and turn him in. At the very least, hopefully Dillon can lock him up for the vandalism to the motel room."

"Rationally I know all that," she replied. "But, Dusty, if it is Frank and he stays true to form, then the real threat isn't to me—it's to you." Her eyes were troubled.

Dusty was touched beyond words that her concern was for his safety. "Don't you worry about me, Trisha. I can take care of myself. I've been taking care of myself for most of my life. But if it isn't Frank, then we need to continue to be vigilant where your safety is concerned."

She gave him a rueful smile. "Are you trying to make me feel better?"

He returned her smile. "I know you aren't going to feel better until somebody is behind bars," he replied. He took a step closer to her. Dusk had fallen, painting her features with a faint violet hue. "Trust me, Trisha. As much as I care about you I would never ask you to stay here if I didn't think I could keep you and Cooper safe."

"I do trust you," she replied. "If I didn't, I wouldn't still be here. I'd be in my car driving to who knows where."

"And that's the last thing I want." Aware that she needed to get back inside, he leaned forward and gave her a kiss on the forehead. "Try not to worry, Trisha. I'll see you tomorrow."

"You know where to find me," she replied. "Good night, Dusty."

He watched until she was safely in the house and then he leaned down and pulled the gun he'd stashed in the top of his boot. He hadn't wanted her or Cooper to see the weapon, but he also had no intention of being unarmed until this whole mess was all over.

Someplace out there was somebody who had left her presents and that same person had potentially trashed her motel room. He had no clue if the person was the man from her past or a man here in town. All he knew for certain was that somebody had her in his sights and there was no way that Dusty thought the man's intentions were pure. In fact, since Dillon had told them about the motel room, Dusty had smelled a festering danger in the air.

To Dusty's frustration, the next week passed without any other news. Dillon checked in several times to let them know that he was interviewing people, but nothing substantial came of any of the interviews.

Each evening after dinner Dusty walked up to the big house to spend time outside with Trisha and Cooper. They played catch with a ball Dusty had bought in town, and pretended to be everything from cowboys to pirates.

Each moment he spent with them only deepened his feelings…and his utter vexation that he could do nothing to solve the mystery that would set Trisha free from the fear.

By the time the week had passed, what Dusty wanted more than anything was some alone time with Trisha. As much as he adored Cooper, he definitely needed some adult time with Cooper's mother.

When Saturday night came, he headed up to the house to surprise Trisha with a plan he and Cassie had concocted in advance. Night had already fallen and he'd waited until he knew that Cooper would be in bed and sleeping.

He knocked softly on the back door and Cassie let him inside. "Trisha is in the great room watching television," she said.

"You sure you don't mind this?" Dusty asked her.

Cassie gave him a bright smile. "What's to mind? Cooper is sleeping and I'm glad to play babysitter so that you and Trisha can have some time alone."

"Thanks, Cassie, I really appreciate it." He followed her from the kitchen and into the great room. Trisha looked at him in surprise. "Dusty, what are you doing here?" Her eyes darkened. "Has something happened?"

"No, but something is about to happen if you're up for it," he said. "You and I are going to have a date under the stars."

Her pupils flared with what could only be pleasure even as a tiny frown danced across her forehead. "But what about…"

"I've got Cooper covered," Cassie said smoothly.

"Go on and have some quality time with your boy-friend. I'll listen for him while you're gone."

Dusty held his hand out to Trisha. "You game?"

"Absolutely," she replied and got up and took his hand.

"Don't worry about a curfew," Cassie yelled after them in a teasing tone as they left the room and headed for the back door.

"Thanks, Mom," Dusty replied and was rewarded by Trisha's giggle.

"Did you have this planned ahead of time with Cassie?" she asked him as they walked out into the warm night air.

"I might have mentioned something to her last night," he replied. "Your chariot awaits." He gestured to Juniper, who stood saddled and ready.

"Oh, Dusty, I've never been on a horse before."

"There's nothing to be afraid of. Juniper is a sweet mount and all you have to do is ride behind me and hang on."

She released the familiar breathy laugh that was filled with more excitement than fear, the same laugh that always fired more than a little bit of desire in him. "The fact that I'm willing to get on the back of that beast should show you how much I really do trust you."

He flashed her a grin and then mounted and leaned down toward her and took her by the forearm. "All you have to do is step on my boot in the stirrup and then swing your other leg up and over and plant your-self in the saddle behind me."

She got it right on the first try and laughed with her success. "See, you're a natural," he said.

She wrapped her arms tight around his waist. "Aren't you a man of many surprises," she said.

"The surprises have only just begun." He took off at a slow pace across the yard, grateful for the bright moonlight that spilled down from overhead. What he wanted was for her to feel like a princess for the night...for her to feel like *his* princess.

He didn't want to talk about old murders or present potential threats. He wanted one night to hopefully take her away from everything but him.

Above the scent of pasture that a light breeze carried, her fragrance of wildflowers and vanilla filled his head and fired a heady rush of adrenaline inside him. Her body pressed warmly against his back and desire simmered inside him. He had no expectations for the night. All he wanted to do was take her mind off anything negative and maybe sneak in a kiss or two.

"It's a beautiful night," she said, her breath a sweet torment against the side of his neck.

"A beautiful night, a beautiful girl...what else could a man ask for?"

"Maybe a cold bottle of beer?" she quipped.

He laughed, loving the fact that she sounded completely relaxed and in the moment. "Actually, I have something better than beer, but you have to wait until we get settled."

The farther they got from the house, the brighter the stars appeared in the sky. Mother Nature was cooperating, with a cloudless night and a pleasant temperature.

He finally came to a halt in a grassy area of pasture where the cows hadn't grazed this year. There were no trees or outbuildings to hinder the view of the perfect Oklahoma night sky.

"This is our final destination." He was almost reluctant for the ride to come to an end. He liked the feel of her body molded against his and her arms tight around his waist.

He helped her down from the saddle and then dismounted and moved to the saddlebags. The first thing he pulled out was a folded soft blanket. "Just stand still and let me take care of everything," he instructed her.

"Far be it for me to protest," she replied.

He took a moment just to look at her. She wore a light pink button-up blouse and denim shorts, and the moonlight danced in her hair and across her features. Her beauty swelled emotion in his chest. The fact that she didn't seem aware of just how pretty she was only added to her attractiveness.

He hurriedly spread out the blanket and as she sat down he pulled from the saddlebags the other items he'd brought for the night's enjoyment.

He joined her on the blanket. "We have champagne and fresh strawberries, both plain ones and some that are dipped in dark chocolate." He unrolled two delicate fluted glasses from a towel.

"You've gone to so much trouble," she exclaimed.

It was well worth it, he thought as he saw the

glow of pleasure in her eyes. He popped the cork on the champagne and poured them each a glass. He dropped a strawberry into her glass and then handed it to her. "That's the way I understand they do things in the big cities."

She smiled at him. "I wouldn't know. This is the nicest thing anyone has ever done for me." She took a sip of the drink. "Thank you, Dusty for all of this."

"Don't thank me," he protested. "I had an ulterior motive of wanting to have you completely to myself for a little while."

They drank two glasses of the champagne and then stretched out on their backs to look up at the stars. "I didn't know the night sky was so beautiful until I moved here," she said.

"They say everything is bigger in Texas, but I think Oklahoma has the prettiest stars in the whole wide world," he replied. He pointed up. "Do you see the Big Dipper?"

"Hmm, and there's the little one," she replied.

For the next half an hour he pointed out the various constellations in the sky. Then he rolled over on his side next to her and toyed with a strand of her hair, grateful that tonight it was loose rather than caught up in a ponytail.

"If you had three wishes on stars that you knew would come true, what would they be?" he asked.

"Not counting wishing that Dillon gets to the bottom of everything?"

"Not counting that," Dusty replied. "I don't even want you thinking about any of that tonight."

She stared upward as if already making the wishes he'd asked her about. "My first wish would be that Cooper is always happy and healthy."

He wasn't surprised that her first thought would be for her son. That was part of what he admired about her. "And what would be your second wish?"

"Probably what everyone wants...to love and be loved."

"And your last wish?"

She turned her head and looked at him. "That you would feed me one of those chocolate-covered strawberries and then kiss me until I can't think anymore."

She almost giggled at how fast he sat up and tore open the container holding the dipped strawberries. She knew what she'd asked for. She didn't care a whit about the strawberry—what she wanted was passion...his passion and her own. What she wanted more than anything at this moment was Dusty.

She'd wanted him from the moment she'd climbed up behind him on the horse, when she'd wrapped her arms around him and felt the heat of his body so close to hers. Her desire had been stirred when she'd smelled the familiar scent of him...a fragrance that not only made her feel safe and secure, but also more than a little hot and bothered.

Despite the fear that bubbled up inside her at all hours of the day and night, she hadn't forgotten the fiery desire he'd stirred in her that evening they had dinner at the café. It had simmered inside her since that night.

He plucked a single strawberry from the container and then leaned over her with the plump fruit between his fingertips. His gaze bored into hers as he lowered it to her lips.

Shamelessly she drew into her mouth not only the strawberry but the tips of his fingers, as well. She'd barely chewed and swallowed the treat when his mouth crashed down on hers.

The sweet of the chocolate strawberry combined with the fire of his kiss instantly dizzied her senses. She wrapped her arms around his neck and pulled him closer, tighter against her as the kiss deepened.

They'd indulged in a game of foreplay for the last week and now she wanted more of him than she'd ever had before. She wanted him to make love to her right now, right here on the blanket under the stars.

He lay half on top of her while they continued to kiss. The only sound she heard was the faint rush of the breeze, his low moan and her own quickened breaths as their tongues twirled together in a frenzied dance.

He placed a hand on her stomach, the heat of his palm burning through the thin cotton material of her blouse. He moved his mouth to the side of her neck where his lips nibbled.

"Dusty, I want you to make love to me."

He froze and then slowly lifted his head to look down at her. There was hot desire in his eyes, but there was also hesitancy. She reached up and placed her palm on the side of his cheek. "The back room of the café was the wrong place, but it's definitely right here and now."

In response he sat up and pulled his white T-shirt over his head and cast it aside. She began to unbutton her blouse but stopped as he placed his hands over hers.

"Let me," he whispered. "I can't tell you how many times I've dreamed of doing this."

His fingers worked to slowly open her top, and as he exposed each inch of skin he bent over to kiss it. By the time he had the blouse completely undone, she couldn't wait to get out of it and her bra and feel his skin against hers.

He didn't stop with her blouse and bra. He unfastened the snap at the top of her shorts and at the same time she kicked off her sandals. When she wore only her panties, he rolled away from her and pulled off his boots and socks and then took off his jeans, leaving him clad only in a pair of dark boxers.

He gathered her back into his arms, and she released a moan of pleasure. He was warm and muscled. How she loved the way he felt against her.

He kissed her again and at the same time his hand covered one of her breasts. Her nipple hardened in response. Everything was right...the moment, the man and the heady emotions that roared through her.

His mouth moved from her lips to her breasts, where he kissed and sucked each turgid tip. Stroking her hands down his back, she felt as if she was truly making love for the very first time in her life.

He continued to caress her, his tenderness, his gentle touch making her feel more beautiful, more cherished than she'd ever felt before.

There was no awkward fumbling, no clumsiness—rather, they moved together with an ease, as if they'd been lovers for years. When he pulled a condom from his jeans pocket she was grateful that he'd thought about protection and had anticipated what might happen between them tonight.

Her breath caught in her throat as his hand slipped beneath the waistband of her panties and down to the apex of her thighs.

"Oh, yes," she gasped as his fingers danced against the sensitive flesh. She reached down and grasped his hard erection through his boxers.

What had begun as a slow exploration of each other became frantic…urgent. He pulled her panties off and then removed his boxers.

His fingers once again touched her intimately and she arched her hips up and dug her heels into the blanket. Her climax took her by surprise, crashing through her with an intensity that left her gasping.

"You're so beautiful, Trisha. I want you so badly." He positioned himself between her legs and kissed her as he slid into her.

She curled her legs around his buttocks, wanting him deep…deeper inside her. He filled her completely. It was a connection of mind, body and soul.

He pulled back slightly and then thrust, creating new glorious sensations. He quickened his rhythm and she matched it by thrusting her hips upward.

Fast and feverish, they moved together until with a deep groan he stiffened as he found his release.

He rolled to the side of her and stroked a finger across her lower lip. She smiled and sighed with contentment. If the stars had appeared bright before, they now appeared utterly splendid.

"How about another chocolate strawberry?" he asked with amusement. "It worked really well for me just a little while ago."

She laughed and gave him a playful smack on his chest. "I've got a secret to tell you—you didn't even need those strawberries."

"And I've got a secret to tell you… I'm falling hard for you, Trisha." His eyes glowed silver as he held her gaze.

"I'm falling, too, Dusty," she admitted. "I wouldn't have let this happen between us if I wasn't."

For several long moments they gazed at each other, any further words between them unnecessary. He moved his hand slowly down her cheek, as if his fingers were memorizing the shape of her face.

"Have I told you how beautiful I think you are?" he finally said.

"Maybe once or twice, but feel free to tell me again," she replied.

He smiled. "You're so beautiful you take my breath away. Everything about you takes my breath away."

"I know it sounds crazy, but I feel like we've known each other forever," she said. "It all feels so natural, so easy with you."

"It isn't crazy. I feel the same way," he replied.

He rolled over on his back and she turned on her side to face him. "I never asked you—if you could have three wishes come true, what would they be?"

"I'd wish that Cooper would always be happy and healthy," he said and her heart swelled even bigger.

"That's so nice. And your second wish?" she asked.

"That you would never know fear again for the rest of your life." He turned over to face her. "And my third wish would be that we could make love again and again." He grinned at her.

"You're such a man," she replied with a laugh.

He sighed and once again reached to toy with a strand of her hair. "I'd love to stay out here all night and sleep with you in my arms under the stars."

She smiled with a touch of regret. "It's a nice thought, but the truth is I should probably get back to the house." Reluctantly she sat up and reached for her panties.

He got to his feet and when he stepped back from her she noticed the glint of a gun on the blanket right next to his boots. It was a stark reality check after the beauty of their lovemaking. She didn't mention it to him and when he was dressed the gun had disappeared once again. He apparently hadn't meant for her to see it.

As they rode across the moonlit pasture to the house, she leaned her cheek against his back and thought again about the gun. The fact that he was armed and obviously didn't want her to know about it only made her feelings for him deepen.

He'd sworn that he would protect her and Cooper,

and the weapon only told her that he meant exactly what he said. She could depend on him. It had been so very long since she'd been able to depend on anyone.

Juniper's rhythmic walk coupled with the emotional wonder of making love had her drowsy with impending sleep by the time they halted at the house.

Dusty eased her down from the saddle and then dismounted and walked with her to the back door. "I hate to tell you goodbye," he said, pulling her close.

"Me, too." She leaned into him as he stroked her hair.

He tipped her chin up and gave her a gentle kiss. "Get some sleep, Trisha. I'll see you tomorrow."

She stepped back from him. "Dusty, thank you for everything."

His dimpled grin flashed. "Trust me, the pleasure was all mine. Sweet dreams."

She went inside and locked the door, but stood and watched as he remounted Juniper and headed for the stable in the distance. He was everything she'd ever wanted, everything she'd been afraid to fantasize might be possible in her life.

Tonight they'd taken a firm step forward, a step that could easily lead to a future of happiness and love. All they both had to do was stay alive.

Chapter 10

Another three days had passed, and on Tuesday evening Trisha and Dusty sat in lawn chairs just outside the back door while Cooper played with his cowboy figures in the dirt.

They'd spent every evening together and each and every minute that they shared only confirmed to her that he was the man she and Cooper wanted in their lives.

But on this night it was her immediate future that weighed heavily on her mind. "I need to get back to work at the café," she said.

Dusty looked at her in surprise. "Why? Has Cassie said something to you about it?"

"No, she's been nothing but supportive and friendly. But I'm not used to depending on anyone, and I can't just sit around here for an indefinitely long time without tending to my finances. It might be inconvenient, but it's a reality."

Dusty frowned. "What about Cooper?"

"I'm sure Juanita would be happy to watch him at her house. The only reason I had her come to the motel to babysit was that I thought it would be more convenient for her to watch him where he had his own bed for napping and all of his toys available to him."

"I like the idea of you being safe right here," he said.

"I like that, too, but it's already been almost two weeks and Dillon hasn't come up with any answers. How long am I supposed to just put everything on hold? Daisy certainly can't keep my job open for me forever and I don't expect her to."

"Is the job really that important to you?"

"Absolutely," she replied. "Oh, I know most people don't aspire to be a waitress, but I love what I do. I enjoy interacting with people at the café and serving them food that makes them happy. Was it what I dreamed of being when I was young…? No, but it's definitely who I am now."

He raised an eyebrow and looked at her with curiosity. "And what did you dream of being when you were young?"

"A rock star, but that didn't work out, and don't change the subject," she retorted.

He grinned and then raked a hand through his hair. "There's only one way I would want you to go back to work and that's if I take you and pick you up each day.

I'm sure you'd be safe inside the café among the other people, but I wouldn't want you driving yourself."

She released a sigh of frustration. The last thing she wanted was to add to Dusty's workload. But she needed to feel as if she was being productive, that she was in control of something in her life. She needed to get back to work.

Besides, the past couple of days Cooper had asked about when he would be able to see Juanita again. The older woman had been a regular part of his life since he was a baby, and it was obvious that he missed seeing her. She was like the doting grandmother he'd never had.

"Never mind," she finally said.

Dusty eyed her with open amusement. "Really? Is that the way you fight for what you want? You just give up that easily?"

"Only when my wants put a burden on somebody else," she replied.

"Trisha, nothing could make me feel like you're a burden," he assured her. "I'll be more than happy to see to it that you get to work and back here safely. Just let me know when and I'll be available."

How had she gotten so lucky to have a man like Dusty in her life? Was it really just some terrible trick of fate? A glimpse of what happiness looked like before it was all stolen away from her?

It was difficult to maintain the negative thoughts as Dusty got out of his chair and joined Cooper in the dirt, their laughter riding on the evening air.

While the two of them played make-believe, it was

impossible not to notice how much they looked alike, with their blond hair and blue eyes. Dusty could easily be mistaken for Cooper's father. The thought welled an unexpected wistfulness inside her, the longing for another baby…for Dusty's baby.

The daylight began to wane, and all too soon it was time for Trisha to call it a night. "I think it's about time to pack up the cowboys and head inside," she said.

"Five more minutes?" Cooper asked.

"Okay, five more minutes and then no arguments," she agreed.

"Thanks, little lady," Cooper replied in his drawling Duke imitation.

"Yeah, thanks, little lady," Dusty echoed with a laugh.

Fifteen minutes later Cooper was in a bathtub filled with warm water and vanilla-scented bubbles. "I love Dusty," Cooper said as washed his knees. "Why can't he be my daddy?"

"Because it's not that easy," Trisha replied.

"Why isn't it easy?" Cooper asked.

"It just isn't." Trisha knew the answer wasn't a real answer, but she couldn't explain to her son that she still feared they would have to leave Bitterroot and Dusty behind. Cooper was too young to understand that fatherhood was much more than just calling somebody Daddy.

She and Dusty hadn't spoken of marriage or happily-ever-after. He hadn't said that he wanted to be a father to Cooper or a husband to her.

"If you don't scrub behind those ears, your cowboy figures might just run away from you," she said in an effort to change the topic of conversation. "They told me they don't like boys who have dirt behind their ears."

"That's silly," he replied and then soaped his wash-cloth and worked it behind each ear.

Later, after Cooper was in bed sleeping, Trisha made a phone call to Daisy and told her that she'd be back to work at her usual time on Thursday. Daisy was thrilled. She then called Juanita, who immediately agreed to watch Cooper at her home, only a couple of blocks away from the café.

Her final phone call was to Dusty. Since the night they had made love on the blanket in the pasture, they'd made a habit of talking on the phone each evening before bedtime.

"What are you doing?" she asked when he answered.

"Thinking about you. What are you wearing?" he asked teasingly.

"I wish I was wearing you," she replied.

"Oh, woman, you shouldn't say things like that when I'm so lonely in my room," he replied in a husky voice.

A blush warmed her cheeks. She had never said anything like that to any man in her entire life. But he made her feel so sexy and desirable. She felt so safe with him to explore all dimensions of herself as a woman.

"Actually, I didn't call to get you all fired up, I

called to let you know that I've arranged to go back to work on Thursday."

"Trisha, you fire me up when you just tell me hello," he replied. "And don't worry about the work thing, we'll figure it all out."

She squeezed her phone more tightly against her ear as the depths of her feelings for him filled her chest. She was madly, crazy in love with him and the need to tell him trembled on her lips.

But she'd loved Courtney and Courtney had been killed. She'd loved her mother, and her mother was also gone, murdered by an insane jealousy whose name was Frank.

When she loved, people died. She couldn't tell Dusty that she loved him until she knew it was absolutely safe, until this madness was all over. "I really just wanted to tell you good-night," she finally said.

"Sweet dreams, Trisha," he replied softly.

An hour later she lay in the dark, thinking about her return to the café. If it wasn't Frank who had come back to torture her, then would she get some sort of clue as to who might be responsible by being back at work and talking to the men who came in?

Would one of the cowboys she served say or do something that would point to his culpability? She hoped so. It might be the only way the guilty party would be identified and this whole mess would finally end.

She hated the uncertainty. She hated just waiting for something else to happen. She wanted this over so she could really move on with her life.

Thursday afternoon the ride in to work went off without a hitch. Cooper was dropped off at Juanita's home and Dusty promised to be back at the café at ten that evening to get them back to the ranch safely.

Daisy greeted her with a warm hug that didn't quite dispel the bounce of nerves inside Trisha as she got back to work on the floor.

Surprisingly, as the afternoon wore on she found herself relaxing, visiting with many of the towns-people who came in and realizing that, shockingly, nobody seemed to know anything about what was going on in her personal life, or at least it wasn't a topic of discussion.

As she went about her work she was reminded again and again of how many good people there were in the small town and how much she wanted to make this her permanent home.

It was just after the early dinner rush when some of the men who were on her radar began to come in. The first was Steve Kaufman, who took his usual booth in her section.

"Trisha, I've missed seeing you around here," he said when she approached him to take his order. "I certainly hope everything is okay with you and your son." His dark eyes bored into her as he placed a paperback copy of *Lord of the Flies* next to him.

"Everything is fine, Steve. I just decided I needed a little mini vacation," she replied. "It was great to spend the extra time with my son."

"That's nice, but I have to confess that I'm glad you're finally back," he replied.

Was he the one? she wondered as she delivered a cup of coffee to him. She knew his wife had died two years before. Had his grief somehow turned him into a dangerous stalker?

Or was Frank somewhere in town with his blond hair dyed black and maybe a scruffy beard hiding his strong features? Surely if there was a stranger in town Dillon would know about it by now. Bitterroot wasn't that big, and he had all of his officers on high alert.

It was just after six thirty when Shep Harmon and Greg Albertson walked through the door. They also sat at a booth in her section. The two Humes ranch hands weren't too bad when they were without Zeke Osmond and Lloyd Green and some of their other cohorts.

"Hey, Trisha, long time no see," Greg said, his slightly plump features uplifted with his friendly smile.

"We were starting to wonder if maybe you'd left town or something," Shep added.

"Why would I do that?" she asked. Had Shep left the things at her door? Had Greg? How she wished she could see into the heads of every man in town to learn who was guilty and who wasn't.

Shep shrugged his broad shoulders. "Beats me. I never try to figure out why a woman does something. What's the special tonight?"

"Spaghetti and meatballs," she replied.

"I'll take that," Shep said. "Daisy makes great meatballs."

"Make that two," Greg added.

Trisha went back into the kitchen to place their orders with the cook and when she returned to the floor, she saw that Zeke and Lloyd had joined Shep and Greg.

With a deep breath for patience, she returned to the booth, where both men gave her salacious smiles that made her want to head to the nearest shower.

"Ah, sweet Trisha, so good to see your sexy self again," Lloyd said.

"Hey, Trisha, are you still seeing that snot-nosed cowboy?" Zeke asked.

"I can't imagine who you're talking about, and in any case it's really none of your business," she replied stiffly.

Zeke's eyes narrowed and Lloyd laughed. "I guess she told you what for, boy," he said to Zeke. "Give me a double cheeseburger and fries."

"I'll have the roast dinner," Zeke said in a surly tone. "And let me know when you're ready to dump that stupid cowboy for a real man in your life."

"Would you like the mashed potatoes on the side or on the front of your shirt?" Trisha replied sweetly. The three other men laughed uproariously.

"You think you're real funny. Well, I got news for you, that just cut your tip in half," he retorted.

"Hell, Zeke, you never tip worth a damn anyway," Greg exclaimed as Trisha whirled around to place the orders.

Once in the kitchen she took a minute to steady herself. Daisy walked over to her with a concerned expression. "Are you okay?"

"I'm fine," Trisha said to her boss. "I just hate dealing with the Humes men. They're all such…such…"

"Jerks," Daisy replied.

Trisha gave her a rueful smile. "The word *jerks* isn't what initially popped into my head."

Daisy laughed. "Trisha, you know they don't have a brain between them. Don't let them get to you."

"I know," she said. But still, she couldn't help regretting her impulsive words to Zeke.

She couldn't help wondering if she'd possibly just baited a man who was already a dangerous creature.

Saturday night, Dusty was in the stables alone, brushing down Juniper after a late-night ride among the herd. As always, whenever he was alone, his thoughts filled with all things Trisha.

He'd been grateful that there had been no issues so far with her returning to work. It felt remarkably normal for him to take Cooper to Juanita's and then drop off Trisha at the café only to return for them both when her shift was over at ten.

Usually on the way to town Cooper kept the conversation fun and light, and when Dusty came to pick the boy up, he was sound asleep.

Dusty would never have believed he would like the way a little boy felt curled up in his arms as he carried him to the truck. He'd never have believed that he would enjoy the sleepy kiss Cooper gave him when he carried him up the stairs and placed him in the twin bed.

Through Cooper he was exploring a part of himself that he never had before…the wonderful world of childhood. Dusty might not have imagined having children before, but now he couldn't imagine not having Cooper in his life, just like he couldn't envision not having Trisha.

Never in his life had he thought about his future as much as he had since the night he and Trisha had made love under the stars. He'd been content living in the bunkhouse and hadn't really considered a different kind of lifestyle until now.

He was ready to make a move. He was more than ready to find a place where the three of them could live together and build their future, but he knew things had happened fast between them. He wasn't sure where Trisha's head was. It was quite possible that she wasn't as all in as he was.

Besides, there were so many things unsettled right now. How could she even think of planning a future with potential danger still hanging over her head? Or perhaps over his?

He was just relieved that she hadn't left town, that she'd chosen to remain here and see how things played out. He hoped she continued to stay, because it was growing more and more difficult for him to imagine life without her and Cooper.

He finished brushing Juniper and moved the horse to a stall. On impulse he pulled out his cell phone and dialed Forest. It had been too long since he'd talked to his friend.

"Dusty! I was just telling Patience this morning that it was time for a check-in with you."

"How are things going in Oklahoma City?" Dusty asked.

"I've never been happier in my life," Forest replied. "I've put an offer on a piece of property just outside town. It has a nice house on it and we're hoping the owner accepts."

"So, when are the wedding bells going to ring?" Dusty asked.

"Patience wants a Christmas wedding and she's already planning all of the details. How are things with you and all the other men?"

"I told you that I finally got up the nerve to ask Trisha out. Well, things have been going better than I ever imagined. I'm crazy about her, Forest, but we have some issues."

"What kind of issues?"

Dusty leaned against Juniper's stall door and explained everything that had been happening. "I just hope she's safe here at the ranch with me watching over her."

"Of course she is," Forest said with confidence. "You're a strong man, Dusty, and there's no doubt in my mind that you'll do everything in your ability to keep the people you care about safe."

Dusty closed his eyes for a moment. He hadn't realized until this moment how much he'd needed somebody to remind him that he wasn't a vulnerable boy anymore. He was a man who could protect his own now.

"Hopefully you and Trisha will be able to make

the trip into the big city for the wedding. In fact, I'd like you to be my best man, Dusty."

Dusty was surprised and pleased. "Forest, I'd be honored," he replied.

"I'll let you know all the details as soon as Patience tells me," Forest said with a touch of humor. "She's definitely the person in charge of this operation."

The two men visited for another few minutes and then said their goodbyes. For several moments he remained against the stall door.

Forest had sounded so happy, and nobody was more pleased for the big man than Dusty. Forest had been such an important person in Dusty's life. He'd not only protected Dusty during those bad days on the streets, but he'd also been a source of support, wisdom and guidance through the years.

He'd just turned away from the stall door when he heard the loud creak of the main stable door opening. He tensed and immediately his hand fell to the butt of his gun in the belt around his waist.

"Who's there?" he called out.

"Dusty, it's me." Trisha's voice rang out bold and strong from the front of the stable. "Where are you?"

"Stay there, I'll come to you." He headed toward the stable door and grinned when he saw her. "What a nice surprise. What are you doing out here this late at night?"

"Cassie told me to get out of the house for a little while, and Tony was just outside and told me he thought you were in here. He escorted me here from the yard."

"So, here I am…and here you are," he said as he wrapped his arms around her and gave her a kiss on the forehead. "Welcome to my world," he said as he dropped his arms from around her.

She gazed around with interest. "I've never been in a stable before. Show me around?"

Her eyes sparkled with pleasure, and as always the scent of her half muddied his mind. Her yellow T-shirt and shorts were like a burst of sunshine, as was the warmth of her smile.

They'd had no time alone since the night in the pasture and what he wanted to do was lay her down in a bed of fresh hay and make love to her all over again. But he sensed that she hadn't come in search of him for a rousing bout of sex. Besides, Brody was still out on his horse and could return to the stables at any time.

It didn't matter—Dusty was just glad to have her all to himself for a little while. "Were you making Cassie crazy?" he asked as he led her down the aisle with the wooden stalls on either side.

"I don't think so. She just told me to take a break and spend a little time with you and without Cooper. I think your boss has a bit of a romantic soul someplace deep inside her."

"I'm just glad to see you," he replied. He gestured down the bank of stalls. "As you can see, this is where the horses are kept."

"Don't let Cooper see this, he'll be asking you to get him a horse," she said wryly.

"Actually, he could start riding any time," Dusty replied and then laughed at her look of motherly horror. "Cowboys start young riding their horses."

"But he's still my baby," she protested.

"And you're an awesome mom," he replied. He slung an arm over her shoulder. "Come on, I'll show you the feed room and Adam's office and then the magic of the tack room."

She fit so neatly against his side as they walked toward the office. They fit together physically as if they'd been made specifically for each other, he thought.

Adam's office was a small room with a wooden desk and several file cabinets. It smelled of horse and hay and stale coffee. "He's usually in here most early mornings, taking care of the books and ordering supplies," Dusty explained.

"He and Cassie seem close," she said.

"We all think Adam has the hots for the boss lady, but so far he hasn't made his move on her. You've been spending a lot of time with her. Has she mentioned anything about Adam to you?"

In the dim light casting down from a single bare lightbulb Trisha's smile was teasing and bright. "Are you thinking of playing Cupid for the two of them?"

He shrugged. "Not really, I just want everyone to be as happy as I've been lately."

"As crazy as it sounds with everything that has happened, I've been happier than I've ever been in my life these last few weeks."

Even in the faint light, he saw the charming blush that colored her cheeks. "I was just on the phone with Forest before you came in. He and Patience are planning a Christmas wedding and he asked me to be his best man."

"Dusty, that's wonderful," she said.

"I feel very honored that he asked me, and of course I accepted. Forest was a huge part of my growing-up years. I'm so happy that he's found happiness. And now, let me give you the rest of the tour before I carry you out of here and straight to my bunk."

She released the breathy laugh that he found so sexy. "There will be none of that tonight, Mr. Crawford. This is just going to be a short visit."

"That doesn't mean that at some point before you go back inside the house I'm not going to kiss you," he replied.

"And that doesn't mean that if you do I'll stop you." Her eyes sparkled with a teasing light. "Now, show me the rest of this place."

He took her into the feed room, with the bins of grain and bales of fresh hay, and then into the tack room, where he closed the door behind them and proceeded to point to the various saddles and explain some of the other equipment.

"But you can't be interested in all of this," he said when he realized he'd been rambling on.

"Dusty, I'm interested in knowing about everything that you do and all the things that are important to you," she replied.

"You're important to me." He leaned back against

the workbench and pulled her into his embrace. "You and Cooper have filled my life in a way I never expected. I can't believe how long I waited to ask you out, how much time I wasted in hesitation."

She smiled. "The important thing is that you did ask me out and I agreed to go out with you."

"And now here we are together." He bent his head and captured her mouth with his. He would never tire of the taste of her, of the sweet heat her lips contained.

She leaned into him, completely surrendering to him and the kiss they shared. Their surroundings melted away as the kiss continued.

He no longer smelled horse and hay and leather. There was just the scent of her filling his head and firing a hot desire through his veins. All sense of time and place melted away.

He cupped her buttocks and pulled her closer against him, his heartbeat accelerating with every breath he took. No woman had ever affected him on so many levels. Physically, she stirred him to heights he'd never known before, but his emotional connection with her was just as strong. This was the woman he wanted forever and a day. This was the woman he wanted to build a life with, to have his children.

He didn't know how long they'd been kissing when she broke the embrace, her eyes registering alarm. "Did you hear that?" she asked.

"What?" He hadn't heard anything but the sound of his desire rushing in his head.

"I heard a loud bang."

He reached for her once again. "It's probably just

Brody coming in from the pasture." He frowned and dropped his arms to his sides as a new scent assailed his nose.

Smoke.

Fire, his brain screamed.

Chapter 11

"There's a fire someplace close. We've got to get out of here." Dusty grabbed her by the hand and pulled her toward the tack room door. He laid a palm against the door, apparently checking it for heat.

The smell of smoke filled Trisha's head and her heartbeat roared into overtime as fear gripped her and usurped the desire that Dusty had stirred in her only seconds before.

He threw open the door and as they entered the main stable area Trisha was horrified by the faint layer of dark smoke that burned her eyes. The horses banged into the sides of their stalls, their high-pitched whinnies panicked.

Was the whole building on fire? How had this happened? Trisha knew how dangerous a fire could be on a ranch. The wooden stable along with the dryness of the area would be like tinder.

The main stable door appeared miles away as the smoke thickened and the horses grew even more agitated. Dusty's tension was evident in the tight grip of his hand on hers as he hurriedly pulled her forward.

Despite the smoke, which appeared to grow thicker, there was no heat that she could discern. But where there was this much smoke, there had to be flames.

"Dusty…are you in here?" a deep male voice called from the main door.

"Brody!" Dusty dropped her hand and instead threw an arm around her shoulder as he rushed her forward toward the door. "We've got fire. I think it's on the west side of the building."

"I saw it when I rode up. Tony and a couple of others already have hoses on it," Brody replied tersely.

Trisha and Dusty stepped out of the stable. Men rushed toward the building from the bunkhouse and the back light on the main house blinked on.

"I'm going to open things up and get the horses out," Brody said and ran past them and into the building.

"I'll go back to the house," Trisha said, not wanting to get in anyone's way. Chaos was everywhere.

"No, stay with me," Dusty replied. His eyes narrowed and he dropped his hand to his gun.

A new fear shot through her. Did he believe that somebody had intentionally set the fire to flush them out of the stable? Did he think somebody might be waiting for them…someone who hadn't anticipated Brody's unexpected, very timely arrival?

Her stomach knotted as her gaze once again swept the night landscape and deep male voices filled the air. A flickering light came from around the side of the building along with the distinct crackle of a hungry fire.

"Let's go check it out," Dusty said. Once again he threw an arm over her shoulder and pulled her tight against his side.

Together they hurried around the corner of the building and there Tony and a couple of other men held large garden hoses spraying water on what appeared to be a wall of fire.

The scene was grim as the flames seemed to grow stronger rather than weakening. Sawyer and Jerrod joined the men with the hoses and used fire extinguishers in an attempt to douse the flames.

Tears burned at her eyes and she leaned weakly against Dusty as the men continued to battle. How had this happened? Was her presence here somehow responsible? Had Frank set the fire in order to get to her…or to Dusty?

She whirled around at the sound of horse hooves pounding the hard ground. Silhouetted in the moonlight were horses running toward the pasture in the distance. She shot her gaze to the left, and then to the right, tensed for any danger that might appear out of the darkness.

Time stood still as the men continued to fight the flames until finally Tony tossed the hose behind him and stepped back from the structure. The flames were now out, but thick black smoke still billowed in the air.

Tony's features were grim along with Mac's and Adam's as they joined Trisha and Dusty. "Definitely arson," Adam said.

"Thank God we got it out before the whole building went up," Mac added. "As it is, it looks like two stalls are a total loss."

"When I first saw it, there was a pile of hay burning next to the building," Tony said.

"Hay? There shouldn't be any hay out here," Dusty said.

"Yeah, well, somebody put it there," Mac said.

Trisha's heartbeat hadn't slowed as she listened to the men. Arson? The fire had been intentionally set? Why? The questions raced through her head once again. Dusty tightened his arm around her. "Has anyone called Dillon?" he asked.

"I'll call him now," Tony said.

"And I'm going to talk to Cassie and let her know what's happened." Adam looked at Trisha. "Why don't I walk you back to the house?"

Dusty dropped his arm from around her. "Go on, Trisha, I'll feel better if you're safe and sound in the house."

"Why don't you come with me?" She'd feel better if he were in the house safe and sound as well and not standing out in the open where something could happen to him. "It looks like the other men have everything under control."

His gaze held hers for a long moment, and in the faint spill of moonlight it was as if he could read her inner thoughts. "Don't worry about me, Trisha. I'll be fine."

With nerves that still pooled hot and electric in the pit of her stomach, she nodded and then together she and Adam headed for the house.

Neither of them spoke until they reached Cassie at the back door. "How bad is it?" she asked as they went into the kitchen. Cassie gestured for them to sit at the table.

"All things considered, not as bad as it could have been," Adam replied. "A couple of stalls are burned, but at least the whole place didn't go up in flames. We'll be able to get a better idea of the damage in the morning. The horses are all out to pasture. Things would have been a hell of a lot worse if Brody hadn't come in when he did."

"It was intentionally set," Trisha said. A new horror swept through her as the full impact of what might have happened struck her.

She and Dusty easily could have been overcome by smoke. The fire could have raged out of control and killed them. The horses might have burst out of their stalls and in their panicked run to escape the danger they could have trampled the two of them to death.

"Thank God Cass had a healthy respect for the potential of fire and made sure that most of the outbuildings had a water source nearby. And now I need to get back out there," Adam said and rose from the chair. "Tony was going to call Dillon. I'll check in with you later after he arrives."

Cassie and Trisha remained at the table as he disappeared back out the door. "You're white as a ghost," Cassie finally said.

"It was frightening, and what really scares me is the idea that I might have brought danger here to you and all the other men." She placed her hands on the top of the table and twisted her fingers together as a deep anxiety fired up inside her. "You do realize that what just happened is probably about me."

"We don't know that," Cassie countered firmly. "We can't know that right now. From what the men have told me, this wouldn't be the first time that a nuisance fire has been set on the property."

"This was way more than a nuisance fire." Trisha appreciated Cassie's attempt to allay her fears, but it wasn't working. She'd just been waiting for another shoe to drop. Despite the couple of weeks of peace, she hadn't really believed that the threat to her—to Dusty—had just magically gone away.

She'd known in her gut that somebody had just been biding their time, waiting for another opportunity to strike. Whoever had set that fire hadn't known that Brody would appear when he had. They'd probably only known that she and Dusty were in the stable all alone.

"Trisha, don't do anything rash," Cassie said softly. "Don't even think anything rash. We don't know for sure what happened out there tonight."

Trisha nodded. "I'm just going to go upstairs and

check on Cooper. I'll be back down in a few minutes." She got up from her chair and slowly climbed the stairs.

She stood at the bedroom door. In the spill of light from the hallway she could see that Cooper slept peacefully, unaware of the drama outside. Her heart swelled at the very sight of him.

Thank goodness he always slept deep and almost never woke up in the middle of the night unless he was sick. She leaned her head against the doorjamb and released a shuddery sigh.

No matter what Cassie said, there was no way Trisha would believe that the fire didn't have something to do with her. Dusty had believed it, too. She'd seen it in the grim set of his jaw, in the way his hand had instantly fallen on the butt of his gun. If he'd really believed it was just a nuisance fire, he wouldn't have reacted that way.

Frightening questions whirled in her head, questions that had no answers. Who was behind all of this? Why couldn't anyone figure this out?

Time to go, a little voice whispered in her head. *Time to run.* Every muscle in her body tensed with fight-or-flight adrenaline. She closed her eyes at the burn of hot tears.

God help her, but she didn't want to go. She wasn't as afraid for herself as she was for the man she loved. She thought of Courtney…of her mother…and the tears burned hotter.

She loved Dusty, but was love enough for them to

face whatever darkness came their way? Or would her love for Dusty ultimately be his death?

Dillon didn't arrive on the property alone. Jim Browbeck, chief of the Bitterroot volunteer fire department, pulled his official car in behind Dillon's in the driveway. Another patrol car added to the vehicles and several officers got out and joined the crowd.

Dusty, along with Adam and Tony and several of the others, watched as they approached the stable. All of the yard lights in the area had been turned on to aid them in their investigation.

"Don't tell me you were involved in this," Dillon said to Dusty.

"He and Trisha were in the stable when the fire was set," Tony said.

Dillon gave a weary shake of his head and then clicked on his high-powered flashlight. "Let's see what we've got."

The men followed Dillon and Jim to the blackened, wet scene. Jim turned on his flashlight and crouched down. "I don't smell any accelerant," he said.

"As dry as everything has been, you wouldn't need any," Dusty replied.

"When I first saw the fire, a big pile of hay was burning. By the time I got the hose, it had leaped to the building," Tony explained.

Dusty fought back the sickness that had been in his soul since the moment he'd first smelled the smoke. There was almost nothing more frightening on a ranch than fire.

Dillon said something, but he was standing on Dusty's left side and his words were garbled. He turned to look at the lawman. "I'm sorry?"

"I said, did you see anyone lurking around when you first went into the stable?" Dillon asked.

"No. If I had, I definitely would have checked them out." Dusty sighed in frustration. He knew the odds of anyone figuring out who had set the fire were slim to none. "I didn't see or hear anything unusual, not until we smelled the smoke."

Dillon looked at his three officers. "Spread out and check the area."

"I'll get some of our men to look around, too," Mac said.

Jim pulled on a pair of fire gloves and began to poke around in the debris. "What have we here?" He pulled out a soggy butt of a cigarette and held it up in the air. "Do any of the men here smoke cigarettes?"

"None of us," Tony answered. "But I know some men who do smoke." His gaze shot off in the distance toward the Humes ranch.

"Zeke Osmond and Lloyd Green," Dusty said flatly.

"Let's not get ahead of ourselves," Dillon replied. "Plenty of men in this town smoke. Bag it, Jim, and we'll see if the lab can pull something off it."

It was nearly an hour later when Dusty and Dillon headed for the house. "Do you think this has something to do with Trisha's secret admirer?" Dillon asked.

Dusty frowned. "Honest to God, Dillon, I don't

know what else to believe. My first thought when I smelled the smoke was that somebody had set a fire to cause us to rush out of the stable. I was half expecting a bullet in my chest."

Dillon stopped in his tracks and eyed Dusty curiously. "Then you believe the danger is to you and not to Trisha?"

Dusty deepened his frown as he stared at the house, where the kitchen light burned bright now that all of the other lights in the yard had been turned off.

"I don't know. I do know that Trisha thinks I'm the one in danger because of the murders of her best friend and her mother—and then there was the big timber rattler in my bunk room."

"What?"

Dusty quickly explained about finding the snake in his bed. "I checked my room a couple of times, but I couldn't figure out how the critter got in."

Dillon released a deep, weary sigh. "Be careful, Dusty. I can't get a handle on anything that's going on right now. None of my men have spotted any strangers in town and none of my interviews have led to any answers. I've never been so frustrated."

"That makes two of us," Dusty replied.

They walked the rest of the way to the house in silence. All Dusty wanted to do now was talk to Trisha. He needed to make sure she wasn't ready to bolt.

She and Cassie were seated at the table when he and Dillon walked in. Trisha was still pale and her eyes shimmered overbrightly.

"Tell me something I don't know," Cassie said to Dillon as he and Dusty sat.

"I wish I could," Dillon replied soberly.

"But the good news is that Jim found a cigarette butt," Dusty said.

"And I'm hoping the lab can pull some DNA results," Dillon added.

"How long will that take?" Trisha asked.

"Hopefully no longer than a week or so. It depends on how busy the lab is," Dillon replied. "I'll have one of the men drive it into Oklahoma City first thing in the morning."

Adam came in through the back door. Dark soot clung to his forehead and cheeks. "The stable is still smoky, so we won't try to round up the horses tonight. I'll order the supplies to repair the two stalls first thing in the morning."

"Thanks, Adam," Cassie replied.

"Cassie, do you mind if I talk to Trisha in the front parlor?" Dusty asked.

"I don't mind at all," she replied.

Together they got up from the table and Dusty led her through the great room and into the smaller formal living room. He sat on the floral love seat and gestured for her to sit next to him.

"All of us men always hated this room," he said. "It was where Cass would bring us when she was angry with one of us."

"Were you in here often?" She sat on the very edge of the cushion as if ready to flee at any given moment.

"Only twice. The first time was when I threw a

firecracker into Sawyer's room on the Fourth of July, and the second time was when I got drunk on moonshine and was too sick to work. I don't know what made Cass angrier, the fact that I was only sixteen and drank alcohol or that I couldn't pull my weight around the ranch the next day. I'll tell you one thing, that was the first and the last time I drank moonshine."

She looked at him searchingly, her blue eyes troubled. "It's not working, Dusty. You can't just sit here and tell me amusing stories and take my mind off what just happened."

He leaned forward and grabbed her hand in his. "Okay, it was scary, but we're both okay and we're going to keep being okay until Dillon has somebody behind bars."

She didn't believe him. The doubts darkened her eyes to a midnight blue. He sighed. "Is this it, Trisha? Is this the way you fight for something you want? You give up so easily?" He repeated what he'd said to her when she'd wanted to go back to work.

She closed her eyes. When she opened them and looked at him once again, strength had taken the place of fear. "I don't want to run, Dusty. But I'd never forgive myself if something happened to you."

"If you leave me now, then *he* wins. Your entire future, Cooper's future will be running from place to place and looking over your shoulder. You'll always be afraid to care about anyone, to stick around for too long. Is that really what you want?"

"Of course not," she replied. She pulled her hand from his.

"Are we having our first fight?" he asked in an attempt to alleviate some of the tension that crackled in the air.

A grudging smile lifted one corner of her mouth. "You have the amazing ability to give me hope just when I'm on the verge of despair."

He reached for her hand once again and was rewarded by the curl of her fingers with his. "We're good, then?"

She nodded. "We're good."

He pulled her up off the sofa and gave her a kiss on her forehead. "Get some sleep, Trisha. Everything always looks brighter in the daytime."

It wasn't until he left the house to head for the bunkhouse in the distance that Dusty once again went on high alert. He pulled his gun from its holster and moved quickly through the night toward the safety of his room.

Once inside, he locked his door and then sank down on the edge of the bed. He believed he'd managed to calm Trisha down for now, but for how long? How much more could she take before she decided to cut and run?

He hoped Dillon came up with some answers sooner rather than later because he now had the feeling that he was not only working against a madman's timeline, but also against Trisha's uncertainty whether he and whatever they might share were ultimately worth the risk.

* * *

Dillon drove through the night with the burn of frustration deep in his gut. As if the mystery of the skeletal remains wasn't enough. He tightened his fingers around the steering wheel.

Even if he did get the DNA results from the cigarette Jim had found, he'd still have to swab every smoker in the town to see if he could find a match. And that was so not happening. He didn't have the budget and he didn't have the authority for such a task. He certainly hadn't wanted to mention that little glitch to Cassie.

Fred Ferguson, the owner of the motel, had called the station nearly every day to see if Dillon had arrested somebody for the vandalism of the room where Trisha had been living. Trisha and Dusty were both depending on him to come up with some answers.

All he'd ever wanted to do was keep the good people of Bitterroot safe from harm, but lately he felt as if he was failing miserably.

For the first time in his career as sheriff of the small town, he doubted his ability as a good lawman. A horrendous crime had occurred over a decade ago on the Holiday land and now Dillon believed that somebody unhinged was walking among them.

A cold wind blew through him, along with the terrible feeling that things were going to get a lot worse before they got any better.

Damn.
Damn!
It had been such a perfect opportunity. He'd been

watching the ranch for days, looking for the chance to get to Dusty and ultimately get to Trisha.

He'd seen Dusty go into the stable alone and his heart had skipped with excitement as Trisha had joined him there. He'd believed he had the perfect plan. Set the fire, shoot Dusty and then in the ensuing chaos, take what was his.

Everything had gone so wrong. He hadn't expected the rapid response of the ranch hands and now he was back in his car, driving aimlessly while the sense of failure burned in the tightness of his chest.

It was time to get bolder. It was definitely time to take a bigger risk to achieve his ultimate goal. He was tired of not having her in his life where she belonged, where she had always belonged.

He'd failed tonight, but that only made him more determined to succeed the next time. She was his future, and he wouldn't rest until she was his forever.

Chapter 12

"Heard anything from Dillon?" Tony asked Dusty as the two of them sat outside Dusty's bunk room door.

"Nothing," Dusty replied. "But then, I didn't really expect to hear anything from him."

The men had spent the two days since the fire repairing the stalls that had been burned. The horses were all back where they belonged and Dusty was now just waiting to pick up Trisha from work.

"There's no way I think that cigarette butt is going to answer anything," he continued. "I don't even know if that fire was set by her secret admirer or by somebody else who has nothing to do with the situation."

"And she hasn't come up with any names of men who she thinks might have some kind of sick crush on her?" Tony asked.

"She has several names, but nobody who has done anything overt to jump to the top of the list. What do you know about Steve Kaufman?"

"Not much," Tony replied. "I know his wife died of cancer a couple of years ago. He's always been pleasant but pretty much keeps to himself. Why? Does Trisha think he might be the one?"

"She's mentioned him along with Zeke."

Tony frowned. "Zeke's name is always at the top of the list when there's trouble. I can't believe he hasn't been put in jail for some crime or another a long time ago."

"Unfortunately, suspecting and proving are two different things," Dusty replied. "At this point as far as I'm concerned every male in town is a suspect." He sighed in frustration and then looked at his watch. "It's time for me to head out." He pulled himself out of his chair.

"I'll see you in the morning," Tony replied.

"Yeah, see you." Dusty put his folding chair back in his room, locked his door and then headed to his truck for the trip to the café and then on to Juanita's to pick up Cooper.

Despite the trauma of the fire, in spite of any potential risk that might come at him, every minute of every day his love for Trisha and her son only grew stronger. Tonight he intended to tell her just how deeply in love with her he was.

He had no idea if she was ready to hear it, but his love had become far too big for him not to want to share. He wanted to move things forward. He wanted to start looking for a house to buy, a place where the three of them could build their future together.

And despite the danger that swirled around them, he trusted that they had a future together. For the first time in his life he believed that happiness, that love was his to claim and that the universe had finally gifted him with what had been elusive until now... until Trisha.

She had to know that he was in love with her, just as he believed that she was in love with him, but he needed the actual words to be spoken between them.

She had to feel his abiding love for her in his every touch, she had to see it shining from his eyes whenever they were together, but it wasn't enough. He needed to proclaim his love out loud.

When he reached the café, he pulled into the parking lot in the rear where staff usually parked. As always the spaces around the back door were full. He found an empty spot four cars down from the door and backed in.

He shut off his engine and narrowed his eyes to look at his watch. The only light back here was the one that shone from a nearby street pole.

He was twenty minutes early. He shoved his seat back and opened his window. He hated going inside too early because he didn't want to pressure Daisy for Trisha to knock off work before her shift was officially over.

September had brought slightly cooler temperatures. Would they still not have answers to anything when autumn passed and winter was upon them?

He shoved away the negative thought. He didn't want anything bad in his head tonight. He just wanted to embrace the future with both arms.

At five minutes before ten, he got out of his truck and headed for the back door. He was just about to open the door when Trisha walked out.

"Hey, you," he said.

"Hey, yourself," she replied with a smile.

"Good night?" he asked as they walked back to his truck.

"Actually, it was," she replied. "What about your evening?"

"It's been fine." They got into the truck to drive the couple of blocks to Juanita's home. "We finished up the work on the stables this afternoon," he said. "And Adam told us Cassie is thinking about throwing a big autumn party and inviting half the town."

"That sounds like fun," Trisha replied as he parked in front of Juanita's.

Juanita lived in a small ranch house on a quiet, tree-lined street. As always, when they got out of the truck, Dusty scanned the immediate surroundings for any potential threat that might spring out of the darkness of the night.

Juanita answered their knock and Dusty followed her down the hallway to the bedroom where Cooper was sound asleep.

Dusty bent over and gathered the boy into his arms. Cooper raised an eyelid and smiled and wrapped his arms around Dusty's neck. "Hi, Dusty," he said.

"Hi, little man," Dusty replied.

By the time Dusty rejoined Trisha at the front door, Cooper was once again sound asleep. Minutes later they were in the truck and headed back to the ranch.

"I spoke to Daisy this evening about possibly changing my work hours," Trisha said.

"Changing them to what?" Dusty asked in surprise.

"I'd like to work an earlier shift so that I don't have to pull Cooper out of the babysitter's bed each night. It wasn't such a big deal when we were at the motel and Cooper slept in his own bed and didn't have to be disturbed, but now I'd really like some better hours for him."

"What did Daisy say?"

"She said that next week when she makes up the new schedule she'll see what she can do for me. Since you've been responsible for getting me to and from work, I probably should have run it by you first before speaking to Daisy."

He cast her a quick glance and smiled. "It doesn't make a difference to me, although I certainly like the idea of you being off in the evenings so that we can spend more time together."

"That's another reason why I wanted to make a change. I already miss sitting outside in the evenings and watching you and Cooper play in the dirt."

He laughed. "I do enjoy playing cowboys with the little buckaroo."

The rest of the ride she talked about her evening at work. "It's always a good night when none of the Humes ranch hands come in."

"I wish we knew what caused the bad blood between Raymond Humes and Cass," he replied. "Even with her gone, I think Raymond encourages his men to cause us trouble."

"Cassie told me she's reading some of Cass's old diaries. Maybe she'll find the answer in one of them."

"Maybe, although knowing about it probably won't change anything," he replied.

He turned onto the Holiday land and pulled down the long driveway and parked. Dusty got Cooper from his car seat and followed Trisha to the back door. Apparently, Cassie was already in bed for the night since the door was locked. Trisha pulled out the key Cassie had given her and unlocked the door.

It didn't take long for Dusty to tuck Cooper into his bed, and then he and Trisha returned to the great room and sat on the sofa. Nerves suddenly clanged in Dusty as he thought of everything he wanted to say to Trisha, the love he wanted to share with her.

"Are you tired?" he asked and reached up to release her hair from the elastic band. Her hair spilled down to her shoulders and he toyed with one of the strands.

She took the elastic tie from him and set it on the coffee table. "A little, but it always takes me a while to wind down," she replied.

"Hmm, you smell like cinnamon," he observed.

She laughed. "I served a lot of apple strudel tonight."

He dropped his hand from her hair. "I've been doing a lot of thinking over the last couple of days."

She looked at him cautiously. "Thinking about what?"

"About us."

"What about us?" Her eyes instantly darkened as if she expected something bad.

He reached out and took one of her hands in his. "Don't look so worried. I've been thinking that maybe it's time for me to start house hunting." He watched her features closely. "I want to find a place where the three of us can live. I'd like to find your forever home, Trisha, and I want to live there with you and Cooper. I'm crazy in love with you. I'm crazy in love with your son, and I want to be your forever man."

He held his breath, waiting for her response. She searched his features and her eyes lightened in hue. "Oh, Dusty, I'm crazy in love with you, too." Her lips trembled as a wealth of emotion flowed from her eyes.

His heart exploded with happiness and he reached for her, wanting to hold her close, wanting to kiss the tremble right off her lips.

She leaned into him and the kiss they shared was tender and filled with the depth of emotion that burned in his heart. He finally ended the kiss and she pulled back from him.

"I feel like I was born loving you," he said softly. "I've wanted to tell you, but I was afraid that you weren't in the same place."

"I'm definitely there with you, Dusty." Her eyes shone with a brightness, a happiness that moved him deeply. "I've never loved any man as much as I love you."

"We've never really talked about what our future would look like," he said.

"That's because I've never really been sure that I have a future."

"You have a future, Trisha. We have a future together and it's going to be wonderful," he assured her. "What I'd like is to find a house in town near the café and I'll continue to work here at the ranch."

He threw an arm around her shoulder and pulled her tight against his side. She leaned her head against him and released a sigh. "Tell me more," she said softly. "Tell me about this wonderful future we're going to share."

"We'll live in a house with at least three bedrooms, one for us, one for Cooper and another that will be a nursery for our babies. You do want more children?"

"At least one more," she replied. "I'd like to have your baby."

Once again his heart swelled, and he tightened his arm around her. "You'll work at the café and I'll work here and then in the evenings we'll eat supper together and watch Cooper play and then go to bed together. We'll get married and laugh and make love and watch our children grow. We'll know the kind of happiness that we've only dreamed about in the past."

He stopped talking as he realized that at some point in his windy portrayal of their future together she'd fallen asleep. He remained unmoving, reluctant to wake her and just enjoying the moment of her at complete rest against him.

The night that he'd asked her out, he'd never

dreamed that he'd be here now with her words of love for him filling his soul. He hadn't been able to imagine that he could love as deeply as he did. He'd been so afraid that his terrible childhood had made him unable to love. He'd been concerned that he'd never know how to be a good father.

Now everything he'd suffered in his life vanished with her by his side. He did love, and he was determined to be the kind of father to Cooper that he'd wanted for himself but never had.

He couldn't believe that he not only had a beautiful woman who loved him, but also a little boy who looked at him as if he were the greatest cowboy, the greatest man since John Wayne.

Are you strong enough?

Are you really smart enough?

The haunting question was like a discordant note in his head. He leaned his head against the back of the sofa and closed his eyes with a resolve he'd never felt before.

Hell, yes, he was strong enough to see them through whatever they might face. The ghosts from his past were just that…harmless wraiths with no more power to plague him.

He was more than man enough to protect what was his. It was the last thought he had before he fell asleep with the woman he loved still snuggled against him.

"More coffee, Steve?" Trisha held the coffeepot poised over Steve Kaufman's empty cup.

"Sure, that would be great," he agreed. "I was surprised to see you when I came in. You don't usually work on Sundays."

"Julia called in sick today. She apparently has some kind of flu bug, so Daisy asked me to come in," Trisha replied. Considering the time Trisha had been off and how accommodating Daisy had been, Trisha hadn't hesitated to pick up the extra shift to help out.

"You sure look happy this evening," Steve observed.

"I am happy," she replied.

"Any particular reason?" He raised a dark eyebrow and studied her intently.

"The weathermen are calling for rain tonight. That's put every rancher who has come in here to eat in a good mood," she replied.

"A good soaking rain would definitely be welcome," he replied. "It's been so terribly dry."

"Anything else I can get for you?" she asked.

"No, I'm good for now." He reopened his paperback book. "Thanks, Trisha."

Trisha nodded and then went behind the counter and put the coffeepot back where it belonged. Daisy walked up next to her. "Why don't you go get yourself something to eat and take a break now that the dinner rush is over?"

"That sounds good to me. I'm starving and you know how much I love your chicken pot pie," Trisha replied.

Daisy grinned. "Everyone loves my chicken pot pie when I have it on the menu. And thanks for covering for Julia."

"No problem," Trisha replied.

While she filled a plate in the kitchen, she thought about the night before with Dusty. He'd told her he loved her and that he wanted to be her forever man. That was the real reason for the happiness she could barely contain.

For the first time since Cooper's birth, a strong hope burned in her heart, a hope built on the love she'd found with Dusty. She truly believed that they would get through whatever they had to face in order to finally claim their forever life together.

Thank God she hadn't run. Thank God she hadn't packed up Cooper and left town when those flowers and the note had been left at the motel. Since that night she'd gotten stronger and more determined to build a real life for herself and her son, and now her future definitely included Dusty.

If only her mother were alive. If only she could meet Dusty and see the love her daughter had finally found. Trisha knew with certainty that her mother would have loved Dusty.

The chicken pot pie had never tasted as good as it did tonight. Work had never been as pleasurable as it had been this evening and it was all because she was confident that she not only loved, but was loved.

It had been after one o'clock the night before when Dusty had awakened her from her sleep on the sofa with him. He'd left at the back door with a kiss and the promise that they were at the beginning of an incredible journey together, one that would last an entire lifetime. It was difficult not to be happy with that promise ringing in her ears, in the very depth of her heart.

She finished her break and returned to the floor, where the rest of the evening remained pleasant. By eight o'clock dark storm clouds stole away the last of the day's light and the talk among the customers was of how badly the rain was needed.

She didn't even mind too much when Shep Harmon, Greg Albertson and Zeke Osmond came in and took a booth in her section. Nothing would bring down her positive mood, not even the cowboys from the Humes ranch.

They ordered pie and coffee, and for a change Zeke didn't hassle her. She served them without any fuss.

"The boys appear to be behaving themselves," Daisy said as she and Trisha once again stood together behind the counter.

"Yeah, nothing short of a miracle, right?" Trisha replied wryly.

Daisy smiled at her. "Speaking of miracles, you've had a new lilt in your voice tonight, a brighter sparkle in your eyes. I warned that dimpled cowboy not to trifle with you."

Trisha laughed. "He's not."

"Then are you going to marry that man and quit your job?"

"Yes, yes, I am going to marry him." Her heartbeat quickened with her words. "We're going to get married and live happily ever after, but don't worry, I'm not going to quit this job. I love working here and plan to continue until you fire me."

Daisy's smile widened. "I don't see that happening. But I'm happy for you. I'd really hate to lose you, Trisha. You're one of the best waitresses I've ever had working for me, and the customers love you."

But somebody loved her too much. Trisha mentally shook herself. She didn't want to think about that right now. She refused to entertain any negative thoughts. She just wanted to exist in the happiness zone that the world offered her right now.

"I hope you're planning a big wedding and I hope you invite me. There's nothing I like more than to cry like a baby at weddings," Daisy said.

"We haven't really talked about the actual wedding plans, but of course you'll be invited," she assured her boss. "Dusty is going to start looking at houses here in town. He wants to get us settled into a place where we can begin our life together."

"I envy you," Daisy said, a wistful glint in her eyes.

"You'd like to get married again?"

"Oh, hell, no," Daisy replied. "I've already divorced two big losers. I don't want to marry anyone, but there are times when I wouldn't mind some hard male body to warm my bed at night." Daisy cast her gaze around. "Unfortunately I'm better at business than at love, and I suppose I'm married to this place."

Trisha smiled at her in amusement. "I have a feeling that if you really decided you wanted a man to warm your bed you wouldn't have much trouble finding someone."

Daisy threw a strand of her flaming-red hair over

her shoulder, and her eyes sparkled with her irreverent zest for life. "You're right. I could probably even bag me some boy toy if I put my mind to it. I just don't know if I want the hassle of having to be nice to somebody when they leave my bed."

Trisha laughed. Daisy was definitely a colorful character, one of the many the town boasted whom Trisha had come to love. Again she was grateful that she hadn't cut and run from this wonderful little town and the good people who lived here.

She bit back a sigh as Zeke motioned for her to come to their booth. "Duty calls," she murmured to Daisy and hurried over to the three men.

"Can we get some more coffee or are you just pretending to work here?" Zeke asked. "And we'll take our tabs, too."

"Ah, Zeke, and here I thought we were actually going to get through this evening with us being nice to each other," she replied.

"Yeah, Zeke…lighten up," Shep said with a touch of annoyance. "Why do you always have to be a jerk to her?" He cast Trisha an apologetic smile.

Trisha went to retrieve the coffeepot and then returned to fill up their cups.

"Shep says I owe you an apology," Zeke said.

"I wouldn't want you to do something you don't feel like doing," she replied as she placed their tab on the tabletop.

"Okay, I feel like it. I'm sorry for being rude. In fact, I think maybe you and I need some sort of a reset button, Trisha. We've kinda been on the wrong foot

with each other lately. I promise I'll try to do better."
He looked at her guilelessly.

She eyed him in surprise. "Thanks, Zeke, I appreciate that."

She left the booth, confused about what he might be up to. She didn't really believe his apology, and there was no way she thought that he was all of a sudden going to become a gentleman. Leopards didn't change their spots, and Zeke Osmond was spotty as hell.

She breathed a sigh of relief when twenty minutes later they left the café. Steve Kaufman also left, along with another couple, leaving her station empty of customers. Thirty minutes more and it would be time for her to go home.

Outside the night sky was dark except for an occasional flash of lightning in the distance. "I just heard we're under a tornado watch," Daisy said as she moved to stand next to Trisha behind the counter. "Its times like this I think about moving to the beach in Florida."

Trisha smiled. "And then you'd have to worry about hurricanes."

"And California has earthquakes. Guess I'll just stay here for the rest of my life," Daisy said. "At least I've got a basement here and a storm cellar at home."

"Hopefully the storm won't get too severe tonight," Trisha replied.

She also hoped that the rain would hold off until they picked up Cooper from Juanita's house and got back to the ranch.

"If Dusty is outside waiting for you, why don't you go ahead and knock off for the night," Daisy said at twenty minutes until ten.

"Are you sure?" Trisha asked.

"Go. It looks like it might storm at any minute, and I'm not expecting a sudden rush of customers," Daisy replied. "In fact, it looks like everyone is heading home to hunker down for the storm."

Trisha immediately beelined to the break room and retrieved her purse. Even though Dusty hadn't come inside yet, she knew he was probably in the parking lot waiting.

She stepped out of the back door and immediately spied his pickup where he usually parked. A rumble of thunder split the otherwise silence of the night.

She'd taken only two steps out the door when a strong arm swung around her neck and she was pulled tight against a hard body.

A wild panic shot through her as the arm tightened against her throat. She reached her hands up in an effort to dislodge the pressure…pressure that was slowly cutting off her air supply.

Help! her brain fired in alarm.

"Dusty!" she managed to scream just before tiny dots danced in front of her eyes and then…nothing.

Chapter 13

Thunder rolled loudly from above as Dusty got out of his pickup and hurried toward the café's back door. Trisha should be getting off her shift at any minute and he was eager to get her and Cooper home before the storm hit.

The last weather report he'd heard minutes before on the truck radio had them under a tornado watch, something that was always taken seriously in these parts of the country.

The last bad storm that had roared through the area had taken Cass's life. That had been last spring, but Dusty knew fall tornadoes could be just as deadly.

The sweet pungent scent of ozone greeted him and reminded him of that late afternoon when the tornado had struck. Afterward Cass's body had been found between the house and the bunkhouse.

The ranch hands believed she'd been coming to warn them of the danger of the impending storm when a tree branch had struck her in the head. He wondered if there would ever come a time when grief didn't ache in him at thoughts of Cass Holiday.

He shoved away thoughts of the tragedy as he walked up the hallway past the break room and into the main dining room, where Daisy sat at the counter with a cup of coffee before her. "What are you doing in here?" she asked.

"What do you mean? I'm here to pick up Trisha."

"She headed out about ten or fifteen minutes ago," Daisy replied with a concerned expression. "Didn't you see her?"

Dusty's heart jumped out of his skin. "No, I didn't."

"Maybe she's still in the break room." Daisy got down from her stool.

Dusty whirled around and headed for the smaller room, hoping…praying she was there and that there was no reason for the sick panic spreading through his entire body.

"Trisha?" He flew into the break room but it took only a single glance to see that not only was the room empty, but the adjoining bathroom was also vacant.

He turned and nearly ran over Daisy. "She's not here."

Daisy quickly stepped aside. "Maybe she's in your truck," she said hopefully. "Maybe you just missed each other somehow when you came inside and she's in the truck waiting for you."

Dusty didn't wait to hear anything else Daisy might say. He raced down the hallway and crashed through the back door and into the parking area.

"Trisha!" He raced for his truck and ripped open the passenger door even though he knew she wasn't there.

His heart beat frantically. He slammed the door shut and gazed wildly around the parking lot. Where on earth had she gone? What had happened to her?

His gaze landed on something on the ground just to the right of the back door. *No. No!* The word thundered in his head as he realized the object was her purse.

He raced forward and grabbed it at the same time Daisy appeared at the back door. "I've called Dillon," she said.

Dusty gripped Trisha's purse tight against his chest. She'd obviously stepped out of the back door. Somebody had been here. Somebody had caused her to drop her purse and disappear. Was she dead someplace in the parking lot? The very thought filled him with an overwhelming nausea.

Lightning rent the black sky followed by an explosive clap of thunder. Dusty shoved Trisha's purse at Daisy and then began to check on the sides and around each parked vehicle in the lot. He moved quickly yet methodically, the panic inside him like a wild, thrashing beast.

She wasn't by or under any of the cars. She wasn't

hidden by the Dumpster. The idea that while he'd been sitting in his truck listening to the weather report somebody had attacked Trisha welled up an impotent rage inside him.

What had he missed? How in the hell had he not seen, not heard that she was in danger? Just when he felt that he was losing his mind, Dillon pulled into the lot, the light on the top of his car swirling red beams that fired through the darkness.

"She's gone, Dillon." Dusty grabbed Dillon by his shoulders when he got out of the car. "I didn't see what happened to her. She came out of the back door and disappeared. She's not here, and we've got to find her before she gets hurt."

Dillon winced as Dusty's fingers bit into his shoulders. "Calm down, Dusty."

Calm down? How in the hell could he calm down when Trisha was gone and he had no idea where she might be? He dropped his hands from Dillon and stepped back, every nerve in his body electrified with the need to do something, anything. They had to find her now.

"Let's go inside, Dusty. I need to ask Daisy some questions," Dillon said gently.

"She doesn't know where Trisha is," Dusty said, vaguely aware that he sounded half-hysterical. Hell, he was totally hysterical. This was his worst nightmare come true.

Cooper. The little boy's name exploded in his brain. "I've got to call Juanita. I need to make sure that Cooper is okay." He yanked his cell phone from his pocket and his fingers trembled as he punched the buttons to connect him to the older woman.

"I'm going to call in some of the other men," Dillon said to Dusty and stepped away from him to make his own call.

Juanita answered on the second ring. "Juanita, have you seen or heard from Trisha tonight?"

"No…why?"

Emotion pressed thick in the back of his throat. "She's missing," he finally managed to choke out. "Dillon is with me at the café and we're all looking for her right now. Is Cooper okay?"

"He's fine. He's sleeping."

Dusty closed his eyes against a crashing wave of pain. When Cooper woke up, the first thing he'd want was his mother. *Dear God, let her be safe and sound when Cooper woke up.* "Can he stay there with you for now?"

"Of course," she replied without hesitation.

Dusty opened his eyes as another bolt of lightning slashed the sky. "Call me if Trisha contacts you. And Juanita, if she comes to pick up Cooper, don't let her take him anywhere."

"Do you think he's in danger?" Juanita's voice held a wealth of concern.

"I don't know what to think," he replied. "I'll see to it that Dillon parks an officer outside your house just to keep an eye out. I'll be in touch."

He disconnected the call and turned to Dillon, who was now off his phone. With panic still trembling through him, he asked Dillon to send an officer to

Juanita's house. Dillon immediately dispatched one of his men.

"We need to do something," Dusty said. Urgency surged a sick high of adrenaline through him.

"I need to question Daisy. We have to find out who Trisha interacted with right before she disappeared." Dillon's voice was deceptively calm.

"We don't have time to ask questions," Dusty replied frantically. His mind spun in a thousand different directions. He wanted officers banging on every door in the town. He needed action rather than words.

"Dusty, we need something to help us figure out who to search for." Dillon grabbed him by the arm. "Let's get inside and see what information Daisy—" The last of his sentence was swallowed by another crash of thunder.

Reluctantly Dusty nodded. Dillon dropped his grip on his arm and Dusty followed him into the building. Daisy had shut down the café. The only people remaining inside were her and four staff members who were cleaning in the kitchen and the dining area.

Dusty felt as if he'd swallowed the storm. Fear thundered through his heart and the very blood in his veins sizzled as if he'd taken a direct lightning strike.

Trisha, where are you? Who has you? Dammit, why hadn't he come inside when he'd first arrived to pick her up? Why hadn't he seen her when she'd stepped out of the back door?

Dillon had only started to question Daisy when Officers Ben Taylor and Michael Goodall arrived. Two lawmen when Dusty wanted a thousand.

"Did Trisha act nervous or strange before she got off work tonight?" Dillon asked Daisy.

"Not at all, she was her usual self." Dark concern shone from Daisy's eyes. "In fact she was in an exceptionally good mood."

"Did anyone give her any trouble?" Dusty asked, unable to stay silent. "Did any strangers come into the café this evening?"

"No and no," Daisy said. "It was a regular night with all of the regular customers."

"I need names," Dillon replied.

Daisy began to list names of the people who had eaten at the café during the evening. Dillon scribbled the names down on a notepad he'd pulled out of his pocket.

Every second that passed was sheer torture. Every minute that crawled by was an agony like Dusty had never known before in his entire life. Even the brutal battering he'd taken over and over again from his own father hadn't prepared him for the pain that roared through him now.

Time was the enemy and already it was as if a lifetime had passed since he'd come inside the café and realized Trisha was gone.

"Steve Kaufman was in as usual," Daisy continued.

"Trisha wondered if he might be her secret admirer," Dusty said. If the widower had or harmed Trisha, Dusty would rip his head off.

Dillon looked at Ben Taylor. "Call Aaron and have him head to Kaufman's house to check things out."

Dusty fought the impulse to jump out of his chair and head straight to Steve's home.

"Three of the Humes men were in," Daisy continued.

"Which three?" Dillon asked. A pulse worked in his jawline.

"Greg, Shep and Zeke were all together. I suppose the only rather unusual thing that happened was that Trisha told me that Zeke actually made nice with her this evening."

Zeke.

The name boomed in Dusty's head. Zeke Osmond, who had seemed a bit upset that Trisha was dating Dusty. Zeke had asked her out and Trisha had rejected him. Zeke was the man who had been on the radar as a potential suspect in both Dusty's and Trisha's minds.

Dusty couldn't contain himself any longer. He jumped out of his chair. The time for questions concerning Zeke's guilt in all of this was over. It was past time for a real confrontation with the man. "I'm going to the Humes ranch."

"Dusty, sit down and let me handle this," Dillon replied firmly.

Dusty eyed the lawman with cold, hard resolve. "I'm done sitting around here and waiting. I'm outta here." Dusty hurried out of the building with a rage slowly growing inside him.

If Zeke was responsible for Trisha's disappearance, then Dusty would know within a few minutes.

If he wasn't responsible, then Dusty would know to look elsewhere, but he had to check it out for himself.

A spattering of rain hit his windshield as he pulled out of the parking lot. *Trisha, where are you?* Zeke lived on the Humes property. Did he have her tied up in his bunk? Had he stashed her someplace else? Where? As far as Dusty knew Zeke didn't own any property around town.

Along with the growing rage, a hollow wind of hopelessness blew through him. *Your fault,* a little voice whispered in his brain. *This is all your fault. You should have known better. You weren't strong enough; you weren't smart enough to keep her safe at all.*

She's gone. You blew it, cowboy. He stepped on the gas pedal and prayed that the inner voice was wrong, that it still wasn't too late to rescue the woman he loved.

Sweet success!

The heady emotion shot right to his head as he gazed in his rearview mirror and saw Trisha prone and unconscious in the backseat. It had taken meticulous planning and incredible risk, but she was finally where she belonged…with him forever.

The chokehold had made her pass out. He'd dragged her body behind a car and watched when Dusty had gotten out of his truck and gone inside the café.

The storm had definitely been a blessing. The

thunder had stolen away the single cry that Trisha had managed to make before she'd passed out.

The minute Dusty had disappeared from view, he'd carried Trisha to his car parked on the nearby street, loaded her inside and taken off.

When he was several miles away from the café, he'd stopped. By that time Trisha was starting to come around. He'd taken care of that with a shot of tranquilizer in her arm. He calculated that she would remain unconscious for four to six hours…plenty of time for him to get to the cabin and restrain her.

Life would begin anew for the two of them. Their pasts would no longer matter. The cabin was stocked with enough supplies to last about a year. He figured it would take her that long to forget her former life and realize how deeply she loved him.

He wasn't stupid. He knew it would take some time for him to win her over. But he also knew it would eventually happen. They were destined to be together, and you couldn't fight destiny.

A light rain began to fall as he left Bitterroot behind. It was as if the heavens were washing away all of the past and there was only the future…his glorious future with the woman he loved.

The rain had stopped falling but a stiff wind had begun to scream around the truck windows as Dusty turned onto the Humes property. A glance in his rearview mirror let him know that the patrol car was still behind him.

He roared past the huge two-story house where

Raymond Humes lived. He knew the men who lived on the property stayed in a building like the one on the Holiday ranch. What he didn't know was which unit Zeke lived in.

After pulling to a stop in front of the wooden structure, he got out of his truck. The police car pulled up just behind him and Ben Taylor stepped out of the vehicle.

"Don't get in my way, Ben," Dusty warned.

"Just don't do anything stupid," Ben replied.

Dusty stalked up to the first door and knocked. He then dropped his hand to the butt of his gun and stepped back. Lloyd Green opened the door. His eyes narrowed. "What in the hell are you doing here?" he asked.

"I'm looking for Zeke."

Lloyd looked at Ben and then back at Dusty. "Is there a problem here?"

"Yeah, there's definitely a problem. So which unit is Zeke's?" Dusty replied brusquely.

"Two doors down," Lloyd replied and pointed to the right with a thumb.

As Dusty moved to Zeke's door, Lloyd stepped outside his room. Dusty banged on the door. Nerves tightened his muscles. Was Zeke here? If he wasn't then Dusty could only assume he was someplace else with Trisha.

He hammered again on the door with the back of his fist, anxiety coupled with a simmering terror clawing inside him. The door swung open and Zeke appeared clad only in a pair of boxers. "What in the hell?" he demanded.

Dusty wasn't aware of consciously making any decision when he pulled his gun and stuck it in the center of Zeke's chest. "Where's Trisha?"

"Dusty!" Ben yelled from just behind him. "Put your gun down."

Dusty didn't blink. He didn't even move. His gaze was focused solely on Zeke, who had slowly raised his hands over his head. "I don't know what you're talking about. How would I know where Trisha is?" Zeke replied.

"Are you her secret admirer? Did you kidnap her from the café? Where have you put her, Zeke? What in the hell have you done with her?" The questions exploded out of him as he continued to hold Zeke at gunpoint.

"The last time I saw Trisha was when she served me at the café. I'm not a secret admirer, whatever the hell that means, and I have no idea what happened to her if she's missing now." Zeke held Dusty's gaze steadily.

Dusty wanted Zeke to be guilty because if Zeke wasn't then Dusty didn't know where else to go, who else to question. Zeke might be many things, but Dusty's gut told him that Zeke was now telling him the truth.

He dropped his arm to his side and put his gun back in the holster and then backed away from Zeke's doorway. "Where are Shep and Greg?" he asked, remembering that the three had been together at the café earlier.

Zeke shrugged. "I suppose they're in their rooms. Shep and I drove home from town together, but Greg was in his own car."

"Get them out here," Dusty said. He wasn't leaving this ranch until he'd checked out all three men.

"Do as he asked," Ben said and moved to stand next to Dusty.

Zeke nodded and walked to the door next to his and knocked. Shep immediately answered and Dusty walked over to peer past the man's shoulder and into his small room. Trisha was nowhere in sight, and there was no indication that she'd ever been here.

Ben's cell phone rang and everyone froze. He answered and listened for a moment. "Thanks, I'll let him know." He hung up and looked at Dusty. "That was the chief. Aaron checked in from Steven Kaufman's house. Kaufman is home and there's no reason to believe he had anything to do with Trisha's disappearance."

The sickness of defeat filled the back of Dusty's throat. What if she'd been kidnapped by somebody who hadn't even been on their radar? What if Frank really had found her and now had her all to himself the way he'd always wanted?

Dusty looked at Zeke and Shep. With Aaron's report it meant that three of the potential suspects had now been cleared. How on earth were they going to find her? How on earth was he going to save her?

"Greg," he finally managed to say. "I need to talk

to Greg and then I guess we'll be finished here." Dusty fought against a sweeping wave of utter desolation.

Zeke nodded and as he walked down the length of the building to the last door, Dusty and Ben followed close behind him. Shep and Lloyd remained where they were.

Zeke knocked on the door. "Greg, open up," he called.

No light came from the small window. Was the man in bed? Was he sleeping soundly despite the thunder and lightning of the storm that had raged overhead?

Zeke knocked again, this time harder. Tension built up inside Dusty while they waited another long, agonizing minute. Zeke reached out and grabbed the doorknob and then turned to look at Dusty. "It's locked, but I don't think he's inside. He would have answered by now."

"Anyone have a key?" Dusty asked, the tension in the pit of his stomach twisting into a thousand knots.

"Just Greg," Zeke replied.

"I can't believe he'd have anything to do with this," Lloyd said as he approached where they all stood. "He's just a good old boy who doesn't have a whole lot of brains."

"Step aside, I'm breaking down the door," Dusty said. He needed to see inside the room. If Greg had anything to do with Trisha's disappearance, then maybe there would be a clue inside.

"You can't do that," Ben protested.

Dusty turned and looked at the officer grimly. "Ben, you'll have to arrest me in order to stop me." He motioned for Zeke to move away and then he lowered his shoulders and slammed into the door.

Pain exploded through his entire body, but he welcomed it as the physical ache momentarily usurped the emotional agony that tore at him. He drew a deep breath and slammed into the door again…and again.

With a loud crack of the jamb, the door finally sprang loose. Dusty burst inside and fumbled for a light switch. A single bare bulb dangling from the ceiling turned on.

He stared around in disbelief. Not only was there no sign of Trisha, but the room looked as if nobody had ever lived in it. There were no clothes and no personal items except a cell phone on the nightstand.

Dusty walked over and picked it up. It was a cheap burner flip phone. He flicked it open, but got no dial tone. He slammed it shut.

"I'll be a son of a bitch," Zeke exclaimed. "Maybe Greg isn't as dumb as we all thought."

"I thought it was kinda strange when he wanted to drive his own car tonight instead of riding with us," Shep said.

"He probably left the phone here so that we couldn't trace it," Ben said. "Give it to me and maybe Dillon will be able to do something with it."

Dusty handed the phone to Ben. Greg Albertson. The name fried in Dusty's brain. "You'd better call Dillon and tell him it's Greg, and Greg better pray that Dillon finds him before I do."

Chapter 14

Headache. Trisha had the mother of all headaches.
It was her first conscious thought and a moan escaped
her. The pain was excruciating.

Something cool and soothing landed on her forehead. Yes, oh, yes, it felt so good. A cool cloth… Dusty
always knew exactly what she needed when she needed
it. She started to reach up to move the material a little
lower, but she couldn't move her arm.

Why couldn't she move her arm? Her foggy brain
tried to make sense of it. Had she been in some kind
of an accident? Was Dusty okay? Oh, God, was she
paralyzed?

No…no, that wasn't right. She'd been at the café
working and there was a storm coming. They'd been

under a tornado watch. Had she been in a tornado? Had the café been hit?

She rejected the idea as she continued to struggle for memories. Yes, she'd been at the café and Daisy had told her to knock off for the night.

She'd stepped out the door. She'd seen Dusty in his truck. An arm around her neck…*can't breathe… help me!*

Her eyelids snapped open and she stared blankly at the unfamiliar surroundings. She was in a small bedroom. There was a chest of drawers, the single bed she was on, and a nightstand. A small window was across the room, only the black-painted frame showing above a sheet of plywood that covered the glass.

Her head began to pound once again as horror surged up to nearly choke her. She not only didn't recognize the room, but her hands were tied to bedposts on either side. Her legs were tied together at the ankles.

Nobody was with her, but the sound of water running came from another room. Who was there? Who had brought her to this place and tied her up?

Danger! It screamed inside her and she bit her lower lip to prevent a shriek of panic from escaping. She stared at the bedroom doorway and attempted to free her arms, but the ropes that held her were thick and strong.

Was it Frank? Had the monster in the closet finally found her and now gotten her back where he wanted her? And what about Cooper? Where was he? Was he safe?

Tears burned at her eyes as she thought of her son. *Please, please make him be safe. Surround him with every angel in heaven.*

And what about Dusty? A new grief pierced through her terrified heart. Was he dead? Had the person who had taken her somehow managed to kill him and then drag her off?

Was it Frank?

Her frantic heartbeat pounded not only in her chest, but also in her ears. Every muscle in her body tensed as the sound of running water stopped.

Who would walk through the door? Would it be the horror from her past or a new horror? Was it Zeke? Had his apology earlier in the night only been a ruse to put her mind at ease where he was concerned?

Heavy footsteps walked across a creaking floor. They came closer and Trisha's breath lodged in the back of her throat. She stared blankly at the man who appeared in the doorway with a glass of water in his hand.

"Good, you're awake." A huge smile spread across Greg Albertson's pudgy features.

"Greg?" Her voice was a raspy croak. She looked at him in disbelief. He appeared as he always did when he came to the café to eat. His jeans were faded and a gray T-shirt stretched across his big shoulders and slightly protruding belly. He looked so...normal, but there was nothing normal about the situation.

"You sound thirsty." He walked over to the side of the bed. "Here, have a sip." He shoved the water glass against her lips. She pressed her lips tightly together, afraid to take anything from him.

"Ah, come on Trisha. I swear it's nothing but plain cold water." His eyes were filled with the innocence of a child.

Her throat was dry and scratchy. She realized she had to trust that he told her the truth. She raised her head from the pillow and opened her lips, relishing the cool liquid as she took several drinks. He pulled the glass away and set it on the nightstand.

"Is that better?" he asked solicitously.

She gave a curt nod. "Greg, what are you doing? Why am I here?" She tried to keep her voice as calm as possible. She had no idea what to expect from him, what else he might be capable of.

He removed a navy blue washcloth from her forehead and smiled once again. "You're here because you belong to me." His brown eyes shone brightly as he gazed at her with an adoration that made her sick.

"You left the flowers for me…the candy and the notes? You are my secret admirer?" She'd served this man a thousand times at the café and she'd never considered that he was crazy, but crazy definitely lit up the pupils of his eyes.

"I didn't intend to stay a secret for too long." He twisted the cloth in his hands and the smile fell away. "I figured I'd take my time with you, prove to you that I'm the man you were meant to be with, but then Dusty moved in on you and I knew I had to step things up."

Dusty, her heart cried out. "Where is Dusty now?" she asked, fearing what he might tell her.

"Who knows? Don't worry, he'll never find us here. But when the time is right I'll find him." He twisted the cloth even tighter around his fingers.

"Why would you want to find him?" Her heart began to drum loudly once again.

He smiled at her as if she were a clueless child. "Trisha, I know the only way you'll be completely free to embrace our life together is if Dusty is dead."

It was at that moment that she realized Greg wasn't just crazy. He was deadly crazy.

"I've already tried to get rid of him twice," he continued. "I put a rattlesnake in his room and hoped he'd get bitten so many times he'd die. I started the fire at the stable. I wanted you and Dusty to run outside so that I could shoot him and take you, but that didn't work out the way I planned. Of course, none of that matters now. You're here with me and sooner or later Dusty will be dead."

His tone was conversational, as if he were talking about Daisy's daily special or the state of the weather, and that only made the fear inside her climb to new heights.

"Where is my son?" she asked.

"I don't know and I don't care. He isn't a part of our destiny. Eventually when you have my children you won't even remember his name. Do you want me to re-wet this and put it back on your forehead?" he asked and held out the cloth toward her.

"No." She didn't want him to touch her in any way.

The fact that he obviously believed that he would eventually make love to her, that he would happily impregnate her, made bile rise up in the back of her throat.

"I don't feel very well. I think I just need to sleep some more," she said faintly.

"It's probably leftover from the tranquilizer I gave you. Get some more sleep and I'm sure you'll feel much better when you wake up again." He began to back toward the doorway. "Call me if you need anything, Trisha. When you do wake up, we can really talk about our future together." He gave her a tremulous smile. "It's going to be so wonderful."

She didn't really start to breathe again until he had left the room. She was in trouble, and Dusty didn't know it but he was also in danger.

Greg hadn't told her specifically where they were, but he'd seemed extremely confident that they wouldn't be found. She didn't even know how many hours had passed since he'd taken her. She had no idea what time it was now.

Were they close to Bitterroot? Or had she been unconscious for so long that Greg had taken her hundreds of miles away from town?

How was anyone ever going to find her? Even if Dillon and Dusty somehow managed to figure out that Greg was guilty, if they weren't on the Humes property and they weren't in Bitterroot anymore, then how would they know where to look?

She tried to pull her wrists free once again and twisted her ankles in an attempt to get loose, but to no avail. A sob escaped her. She quickly pressed her lips together. She didn't want Greg to hear her cry. She didn't want him coming back into the room.

She realized that she couldn't depend on anyone riding to her rescue. Somehow, someway she had to figure out how to outsmart and outplay a madman.

Dusty sat in the café with a cup of coffee before him. Daisy had opened up the place for the night to serve as headquarters for the officers and volunteers who were searching for Greg and Trisha.

The night had crept by in agonizing increments of time as everyone tried to figure out where Greg could have gone. He had no immediate family members still alive, and he'd lived in the bunkhouse at the Humes ranch for the past ten years.

He owned no property that Dillon could find and even though he'd put out a BOLO for Greg's car, nothing had come of it yet.

The rising sun was a soft, faint glow in the sky, and Dusty couldn't believe that an entire night had passed without Trisha being back safe and sound in his arms.

"Dusty, you should eat something," Tony said as he sat down next to Dusty at the table. The men from the Holiday ranch had been out all night, driving the streets and trying to help. "Daisy is serving up breakfast."

"I can't eat," Dusty replied. He had a ball so big in his belly, so tight in his chest, he wasn't even sure he could choke down the coffee that was quickly cooling before him.

Tony placed a hand on Dusty's shoulder. "You've got to stay strong, Dusty. When we find her she's probably going to need you more than ever."

Dusty was grateful that his friend hadn't said *if* they found her but rather *when*. He'd take all the optimism he could get right now, because a bitter hopelessness blew through his entire body.

Too much time had passed. They had nothing to go on, no place to search that hadn't already been done. Greg Albertson had managed to disappear like a ghost in the night, taking Trisha with him.

Greg was a Bitterroot native. His parents had died when he was nineteen and it was then he'd moved to the Humes ranch to live and work. He had no ties to any other city that Dillon could find. He didn't do social media and his cheap cell phone had been disconnected two days before.

The slightly overweight man with the pleasant features and slightly goofy smile had fooled them all. He'd even managed to dupe the men he'd worked and lived among for years. Greg was obviously much smarter, much more cunning than any of them had given him credit.

Was Trisha still alive? Dusty had to believe that she was, otherwise he would descend into a darkness the likes of which he'd never known.

Until he saw her body, until a coroner confirmed that she was really dead, he'd never give up hope. She had to be alive. Cooper needed his mother and Dusty needed his woman.

"Are you sure you don't want something to eat?" Tony asked. "Maybe a pancake or some eggs?"

Dusty shook his head. "In a couple of hours I need to go to Juanita Gomez's place. Cooper will be waking up and he'll want to know why his mother isn't there. If she can't be there for him, then I need to be."

"What are you going to tell him?" Tony asked.

"I don't know." He curled his fingers around his coffee mug, feeling as if he needed to hang on to something as he thought about Cooper. How did you tell a three-year-old that his mother had been kidnapped? How did you tell a little boy that his mother was gone and nobody knew how to find her?

"Let me know if there's anything that I can do," Tony said.

Dusty nodded and Tony got up and joined several other men on the opposite side of the room. He took a drink and fought against the tears that pressed hot behind his eyes.

He couldn't break down now. He couldn't succumb to his emotions. He wasn't a sniveling punk anymore. He was a man and he had to remain strong.

He downed the last of the coffee and then got up and walked over to Dillon. "Now that the sun is coming up, I'm going to take a drive around town. You'll call me if something breaks?"

Dillon nodded. "Of course I will. Dusty, I've got all the men out on the streets. I'm doing everything that I can."

"I know. I'll be back later." He turned and left the café and headed for his truck. The only hint that a storm had briefly flown through the night before was the cooler temperature and a fresh scent.

He got into his truck and sat for a long moment. He dropped his forehead to the steering wheel as he fought against the exhaustion of a night with no sleep.

Sooner or later he knew he'd have to crash, but at the moment he couldn't imagine sleeping with Trisha still gone. He started his engine and pulled out of the parking lot.

He had no destination in mind. He'd just needed to do something more than sit around and wait. The streets were quiet and he drove slowly, peering at each house that he passed.

Where are you, Trisha? Where has he taken you? Dusty was in his worst nightmare and he didn't know how to wake up. He drove aimlessly, his heart in his throat, for almost two hours. He finally parked on a side street and dug his cell phone out of his pocket.

Juanita answered on the first ring. "Is he awake?" Dusty asked.

"Yes, and asking for his mother. I don't know what to tell him." Her voice was soft, as if Cooper was nearby. "Is there any news at all?"

"Nothing," he replied flatly. "Can you keep him longer?"

"He's welcome to stay here for as long as is needed."

"Do you mind if I come by and have a talk with him?"

"I think he'd like that. He's asked for you, too," she replied.

"I'll be there in five minutes." Dusty disconnected the call and tucked his phone back in his pocket. What was he going to say to Cooper? There were no words to explain this horrible adult situation to a little boy.

Minutes later he pulled up in front of Juanita's home, his heart heavier than it had ever been. What could he possibly tell Cooper that would keep him from being afraid when Dusty himself was so afraid?

Juanita greeted him at the front door. "He's in the kitchen finishing up breakfast," she said as she let him inside.

Dusty walked through the small tidy living room and entered the kitchen, where Cooper sat at the table. The air smelled ridiculously normal—of bacon and eggs and toast.

"Dusty!" Cooper slid off his chair and ran to Dusty and hugged him around the waist.

"How's my little man this morning?" Dusty asked when Cooper released him.

"I spent the whole night here. You and Mommy didn't come to get me to take me home. Why didn't you come and get me, Dusty?"

Dusty crouched down and pulled him close. Cooper gazed at him with big, guileless eyes. "Your mommy got lost."

Cooper frowned. "She's lost? How did she get lost?"

"I'm not sure, but I'm looking for her. I'm doing everything that I can to find her."

Cooper placed his hands on either side of Dusty's face. "But you're gonna find her, right, Dusty?" He grinned at Dusty with clear confidence shining from his bright blue eyes. "You'll find her because you're the best cowboy since the Duke."

The emotion that Dusty had choked back throughout the endless night suddenly overwhelmed him. He pulled Cooper into a hug as tears blurred his vision. No matter what happened, he would do everything possible to be the man in Cooper's life.

He sucked back the tears and released his hold on Cooper. "Will you be okay here with Juanita until we find your mom?" he asked.

Cooper leaned closer to him. "I'd rather go home with you," he said in a loud whisper.

"I'd like that, but I need to keep looking for your mommy," Dusty replied.

"Then okay. I can stay here. But will you come and see me again?"

"I sure will." Dusty stood. He needed to get out before he completely lost it. Cooper's utter trust shone from his eyes, and Dusty knew he'd never forgive himself if he didn't somehow, someway bring Trisha home to the son who needed her.

Minutes later he was back in his truck and he couldn't staunch the tears that coursed down his cheeks. This was his fault. He'd failed her. He'd failed Cooper.

What would happen to Cooper if Trisha didn't come home? Somewhere out there was a biological father who might raise his head to claim his son. The thought of Trisha's monster having custody of Cooper horrified Dusty.

Once again he lowered his head to the steering

wheel as deep sobs exploded from him. He could no longer fight against the utter despair.

Trisha, we need you, his heart cried out, causing the tears to continue to flow. But he was so afraid that this wasn't going to be a happy ending for anyone.

Chapter 15

"Breakfast!"

Greg's cheerful voice pulled Trisha from an exhausted sleep. He carried a tray and placed it across her middle on the bed. "There's nothing better than a hearty breakfast to start a new day."

She stared at him dully. Breakfast? That meant it was morning and she'd been missing for an entire night. She looked at the bacon and scrambled eggs on the tray. She wanted to throw up. He left the room and then returned with a straight-back chair and put it next to the bed and sat.

"I'm not hungry," she said.

"But you have to eat," he protested. "You don't want to get sick. Besides, I went to all of this trouble just for you."

She didn't care about the trouble he'd gone to, but he was right. The last thing she wanted to do was get sick or get weak. If either happened then she'd never figure out a way to escape this madness.

"It's going to be difficult to eat with my hands tied," she said, hoping that he would release her from the ties that bound her.

"Don't worry. I'm going to feed you." He picked up a fork from the tray and stabbed at the scrambled eggs. "I'll always take care of you, Trisha."

Grudgingly she opened her mouth and took the eggs off the fork. She chewed and swallowed, fighting against a wave of nausea. "Greg, you need to let me go. I'm sure a lot of people are looking for you by now."

"They aren't going to find me. Nobody knows about this cabin." He held out another forkful of eggs, but she shook her head, knowing that she couldn't take another bite without getting sick.

"Sooner or later you'll have to leave here to get food or whatever and somebody will see you," she said.

He set the fork down and then leaned back in the chair and grinned at her. "You know, it's amazing what kind of food you can get nowadays from all the crazy doomsday places. They call themselves preppers…people who are preparing for the fall of society and anarchy. I've got plenty of food here that has a twenty-five-year shelf life. We've got a well for water and I can always bag some rabbits and such for fresh meat. We'll be fine without me ever having to go to a store."

His words only increased the nausea. "I need to go to the bathroom." Surely he wouldn't bring her a bedpan.

He picked up the tray and placed it on the floor next to the bed. "I'm going to untie you, but don't try anything, Trisha. Please don't make me mad. Don't make me hurt you."

Fear tasted coppery and bitter, she thought as she saw the hint of menace in his eyes. He was big enough, strong enough that he could easily snap a bone in her body and keep her bedridden and helpless for a very long time.

He untied her ankles first and then moved to her wrists. She gasped in relief when she was free. He grabbed her by the upper arm and pulled her from the bed.

She wanted to jerk away from his touch, to run for the nearest door or window, but she did neither. She couldn't afford for him to hurt her and she needed to get the layout of the cabin before she could possibly plan how to escape.

The last thing she wanted was to do something risky or rash. She had to be patient if she was ever going to get an opportunity to get away from him.

They left the bedroom and entered a room that was a combination living area and kitchen. A potbellied stove stood in one corner and a single window displayed nothing but thick woods outside.

The bathroom was tiny, with only a shower stall, the commode and a pedestal sink. A small window was high above the stool and she eyed it longingly but knew she probably couldn't fit through it.

"I'll give you a few minutes," he said. He closed the door and instantly her tears began to flow. She was trapped with a lunatic who believed she was his destiny.

Thank goodness Cooper wasn't here with her. But even this thought was little comfort. Would she ever hold him again? Would she ever see his beautiful smile, hear his happy talk about cowboys and the Duke again? She couldn't think about him. It hurt too much. She had to focus on how she was going to get out of here.

There was no medicine cabinet that might hold something she could use as a weapon. There wasn't even a mirror she could break and use to cut him. Her tears began to fall once again.

Minutes later she left the bathroom and Greg was instantly by her side. "You need to go back into the bedroom and finish your breakfast," he said.

"I'm really not hungry. Can't I just sit in here with you?" She pointed to the sofa and forced a smile. "Please, Greg."

He frowned and then nodded. "Okay, we'll sit in here for a little while." He walked her to the sofa and sat next to her.

"Where is this place?" she asked, even as her mind whirled, seeking any potential escape route. Greg didn't appear to have a gun on him, but he was a big man and she knew there was no way she could physically overwhelm him long enough to get out of the front door.

"We're a little over a hundred miles from Bitterroot," he replied.

A hundred miles. Her heart sank. She'd hoped they were close to the town, where Dillon and Dusty and others would be searching for her. A hundred miles might as well be a thousand…a million.

"Nobody is going to find us, Trisha, and eventually you'll come to realize that we were meant to be together. I've waited a long time for this…for you. I've gone to a lot of trouble to make this happen."

"Did you trash the motel room?"

He gave her a rueful grin. "Guilty as charged. I saw Dusty taking off with you and I'll admit, my anger got the best of me."

Rage. Dillon had said that it had been obvious an enormous rage had exploded inside the motel room. The last thing she wanted was for that rage to be directed at her.

Greg's smile slowly fell away. He gazed at her with an intensity that heightened the fear that already raced through her. "Don't you get it, Trisha? I'll do anything to keep you with me. I'll do whatever it takes to make sure you're mine until the day you die."

Goose bumps rose up on her arms. She'd been so afraid that Frank would find her that she'd never recognized that the affable, overweight cowboy she'd served so many times in the café was the real monster.

It was just after noon when Zeke walked through the café's front door. Dusty frowned as he approached his table. If he'd come here to start trouble, Dusty would punch him out without a second thought. He was in no mood for any of Zeke's crap.

Zeke threw himself into the chair opposite Dusty. "I know you and me haven't always seen eye to eye, but I've been racking my brain and thinking about every conversation I ever had with Greg."

Dusty leaned forward. "And?"

"And Greg mentioned a hunting cabin that belonged to some cousin of his that wasn't too far from here. He spent time there when he was a kid and he told me that someday he'd retire there and live off the land."

A burst of adrenaline fired through Dusty. "Where is the cabin? Can you be more specific? Think, Zeke, this is a matter of life or death."

Zeke frowned. "If I'm remembering right, I think he said it was someplace around Rush Springs."

"Dillon." Dusty yelled to the man seated at a nearby table with a laptop in front of him and then looked back at Zeke. "Do you remember this cousin's name?"

"Bailey... Bailey something. I don't know the last name. Greg hasn't mentioned the cabin for a long time. I don't know if he was just talking a line of bull or not, but I figured I'd better tell somebody about it."

Dillon joined them at the table and Zeke repeated what he had just told Dusty. "Let me make some calls and see what I can find out," Dillon said when Zeke had finished.

As Dillon left the table, Dusty and Zeke stood, as well. "Thanks, Zeke," Dusty said.

Zeke shrugged. "I hope it pans out."

He left the café and Dustybegan to pace as he waited for Dillon to come up with enough information that they would know exactly where to go.

For the first time since Trisha had disappeared, a modicum of hope jumped into his heart. Was this it? Was this the break they needed to find her?

He was ready to jump in his truck and drive to the tiny town of Rush Springs and beat the bushes and bang on doors, but he knew without more information it would probably be a futile search.

"Got it," Dillon exclaimed. "Bailey Summers owns a cabin set on ten acres just south of Rush Springs."

Dusty headed for the door, but stopped as Dillon grabbed his arm. "I've got this, Dusty. It's my job."

"Yeah, well, she's my woman and nothing is going to stop me from going to get her." Dusty wasn't about to stay here and cool his heels and wait for anyone else to rescue her. He needed to find her.

Dillon released his hold on him and nodded. "Okay, then you ride with me and we do things my way."

"We're wasting time."

"Ben… Michael…follow me," Dillon said, and then he and Dusty left the café and hurried toward Dillon's patrol car.

About an hour and a half, that's how long it would take to get to Rush Springs. Millions of things could happen in that amount of time, Dusty thought. But then again, a million things might have already happened in all the time that Trisha had already been gone.

Once they were on the road, Dusty was grateful

that Dillon used his flashing lights to move the traffic aside and let them speed along.

Were they already too late? So much time had already passed. If Zeke hadn't remembered a random conversation from the past with Greg, they'd still be sitting around the café and wouldn't have a lead to follow.

Thankfully, Dillon remained silent. Dusty didn't feel like talking. He was too deep in his own head. Memories of time spent with Trisha haunted him. Thoughts of a motherless Cooper tormented him.

The miles clipped by and with each one the tension in him twisted tighter. If they confronted Greg, would he pull some sick kind of murder/suicide? Was he so obsessed, so mentally deranged that he believed if he and Trisha died together then they would spend eternity together?

Are you smart enough?

Are you strong enough?

The familiar words whispered in his head. He and Dillon and the other men had to be smart enough to get Trisha out of the cabin before Greg could do anything crazy…if he hadn't already.

"We're to meet with Rush Springs' chief of police, Able Grant, when we arrive in town," Dillon said, breaking the long silence that had reigned between them for the past sixty miles. "He'll have information about the lay of the land and hopefully the interior of the cabin to give us a better idea of what we might face."

"I just want to get into that cabin sooner rather than later," Dusty replied tersely.

"You do realize that it's possible we're on a wild goose chase."

"I refuse to believe that," Dusty replied. He had to trust that this was right, that within the next half an hour or so he'd hold Trisha in his arms once again. To think otherwise would destroy him.

Twenty minutes later Dillon pulled into a parking space in front of the Rush Springs Police Department. Ben, with Michael in the passenger seat, pulled his patrol car in next to them.

The four of them got out of their vehicles and entered the small brick building. Dusty's stomach was knotted so tight he felt ill. They were close now. Was this right? Was Trisha really in a cabin owned by Greg's cousin? Both Greg and Trisha were gone…this was the only thing that finally made sense.

Chief of Police Able Grant was a tall, thin man who greeted them soberly. "The property is heavily wooded and everyone here in town thought the cabin had been abandoned a long time ago. It's basically a rustic two-room cabin with a bathroom. There's also a fairly large shed nearby. So, how do you all want to play this?"

"Hopefully, we have the element of surprise on our side and can go in hard and fast," Dillon said. "The last thing we want is for this to turn into some sort of a hostage situation. We don't know the true mental state of the perp."

A hostage situation… The words shot a new fear

through Dusty. He couldn't allow that to happen. The very thought pooled an even worse feeling in his stomach.

"We're wasting time," Dusty said. It was already after four in the afternoon and he couldn't stand the thought of another night without Trisha…without answers. Besides, the darkness might only make things more difficult for everyone involved.

"There are two entrances onto the land," Able said. "The best approach is going to be from the back entrance. I'll take you there and we can figure out a game plan once we're on the property."

Minutes later Dillon and Dusty were back in Dillon's car and following Able and another officer in his vehicle. Ben and Michael brought up the rear.

Six men to take down one nut, Dusty thought. Still, the numbers didn't matter. Ultimately Greg held all the power as long as he had Trisha in his grasp.

They hadn't gotten far out of the town when Able turned off on a gravel road. Dusty sat forward, straining against the seat belt as he anticipated the potential battle ahead.

The only thing that mattered was getting Trisha out safe. Dusty wouldn't hesitate to give his own life to assure her safety. She'd survive if something happened to him, but Cooper needed his mother and right now that was really all that was important.

They passed a dirt road on the right and Able pulled to the side of the road just ahead of it. The others parked behind him and got out of the cars.

"The cabin is just up that road on the left. The shed

is on the right," Able said softly. The only other sound was the cheerful trill of birdsongs from the trees and the frantic beat of Dusty's heart.

He itched to run through the woods and attack the cabin with all the force that he possessed. He wanted to beat Greg Albertson until the man no longer knew his own name. More than anything he wanted to hold Trisha close against him and feel her heart beating against his own.

"Since we don't know with absolute certainty that Trisha is inside that cabin, use nonlethal force. If she isn't here, we may still need him to lead us to her," Dillon said.

"I'll have Officer Dunhill check out the shed," Able said.

Dillon nodded. "Michael and Ben, you two remain at the back of the cabin. Able and I will make our way around to the front. Keep covered—we have no idea what kind of weapons he might have, and the last thing we want is for him to see us coming," Dillon said.

Dusty didn't wait to hear any more. He took off through the woods, his gun gripped tightly in his hand. If they were wrong and Greg wasn't here, then he feared that Trisha would be lost forever.

The trees were thick and provided plenty of cover. He darted between them until the cabin came into view. Relief whooshed out of him on a sigh as he recognized Greg's car parked behind the small wooden structure.

There was no back door and only two windows,

one that appeared to be in a bedroom and another small one he could only assume was in the bathroom.

Where was Trisha? Was she still alive? Surely Greg hadn't gone to all the trouble of kidnapping her and coming here if his intention was to kill her. Was she someplace inside the cabin or locked up in the shed?

He was vaguely aware of the other men darting from tree to tree around him. Where was Greg? Was he standing at a window and looking outside? Was he anticipating trouble?

Trouble had arrived, Dusty thought grimly as he moved closer to the cabin. The birds had quieted their songs and an unnatural silence filled the air.

He gripped his gun more firmly as he raced from a tree to flatten his body against the cabin just next to the larger of the two windows. If he could just peek inside he would hopefully get a glimpse of Trisha or Greg. He needed to know where the two of them were located in the cabin.

Dillon joined him and Dusty motioned toward the window. Drawing a deep breath, he moved his head enough that he could look inside.

He swallowed his frustration when he realized that the window was boarded up, making it impossible for him to see anything indoors.

He turned to Dillon and shook his head, then indicated with a hand that he was going around the side of the building. Dillon moved in the opposite direction.

Crouching low, Dusty turned around the corner

to the front of the cabin. Just to his left was a larger window and beyond that was the front door.

So close now. Staying low, he peeked into the corner of the window. Greg was stretched out on the sofa with his eyes closed and there was no sign of Trisha.

Dusty didn't wait for instructions. He barely glanced at Dillon, who had appeared at the opposite corner of the place. Dusty crawled past the window and then stood in front of the wooden door that would take him inside..

Holding his breath, he put his hand on the doorknob and slowly twisted. He was shocked to discover that it wasn't locked. Apparently, Greg was so sure that he wouldn't be found here he hadn't bothered to lock it.

That was his last thought as he burst through the door. Instantly Greg leaped up from the sofa and ran toward a nearby doorway. Realizing he couldn't shoot the man without knowing for sure if Trisha was here, Dusty holstered his gun and threw himself on Greg's back.

He wrapped an arm around Greg's throat. Greg roared like an enraged bull and whirled out of the doorway and banged backward into the nearest wall in an attempt to dislodge Dusty.

Pain shot through Dusty at the hard contact with the wall, but he didn't loosen his hold. He had to take the man down. He had to win—there was no other option.

He tightened his arm, hoping to choke the big man,

but once again Greg angrily smashed him against the wall. With a groan Dusty slid off his back.

Greg grabbed Dusty by the front of the shirt and the two men tumbled to the floor. Dusty smashed his fist into Greg's jaw but couldn't dodge Greg's upward thrust that hit him square in the eye.

It was easy for Dusty to ignore the excruciating pain. He'd been born and bred to a world where his body had been broken and abused on a regular basis.

Once again he slammed his fist into Greg's face, this time hitting him in the nose. Blood spurted out of Greg's nostrils.

"Dusty!" Dillon's voice barely penetrated through Dusty's brain. "Dusty, get off him."

A scream from the next room fired both certainty and a new rage in Dusty. Greg bucked him to the side and as the two men scrambled to their feet, Dusty pulled his gun.

"Blink an eye and I'll kill you," he warned the big man, who was tense and poised to attack.

"Dusty, put your gun down. We'll take it from here," Dillon said.

"Pull the trigger," Greg shouted.

"Dusty…" Dillon's voice rang out.

"She's mine," Greg exclaimed and then laughed. "If you don't kill me now then I'll come for her again and again. I'm nothing without her."

"Dusty!" Trisha yelled from the next room.

A cold calm descended on Dusty, driving back the killing rage. His need to get to Trisha—his love for her was far greater than his desire to put a bullet between Greg's eyes.

He holstered his gun, and while Dillon and the other men rushed forward, he ran for the doorway toward Trisha.

His desire to shoot Greg once again exploded in him upon seeing Trisha tied to the bed. She gasped his name over and over again, tears coursing down her face as he ran to her side.

"It's okay now," he said as he worked frantically to untie her. "I'm here now and you're safe, Trisha."

When she was finally freed of the ropes, he gathered her into his arms and picked her up from the bed. She wrapped her arms around his neck and continued to weep against his shoulder as he carried her out of the bedroom.

Greg stood in handcuffs between Dillon and Able. Blood still trickled out of his nose and his eyes still shone with madness. "Trisha, tell them…tell them that you belong to me. We belong together. You'll see that he isn't right for you."

"Put me down," Trisha said, her voice suddenly strong and sure.

Dusty set her feet on the floor. She walked over to Greg, raised a hand and slapped him hard across the face. Her entire body shook as she faced the man who had taken her from everything, from everyone she loved.

"You could have kept me tied up here for a hundred years and I never would belong to you," she said passionately. "I belong to Dusty. He's my destiny and that would have never changed."

"That's not true," Greg protested. "You would have grown to love me, Trisha."

"Shut up," Dillon said and then turned to Ben and Michael. "Take him. Get him out of here."

Once Greg was taken outside, Trisha walked back to Dusty and leaned into him and swiped the last of the tears from her eyes.

"Thank God you found me. He was waiting for me just outside the café." She turned slightly to look up at Dusty. "I saw you in your truck and when he grabbed me I screamed for you, but I guess you didn't hear me."

"We can talk about it all on the ride back to Bitter-root," Dillon said.

"We'll do the wrap-up here and I'll send you a report," Able added.

Dusty listened absently as the two lawmen talked and Trisha continued to lean against him. She was safe and Greg would be going to prison for a long time.

He had no doubt that she and Cooper had a wonderful future ahead of them, but he also knew with painful clarity that their future wouldn't include him.

Chapter 16

Trisha awoke to late-morning sun drifting through the curtains at the bedroom window. She started to jump up, her first thought of her son, but then she remembered that Cassie had told her the night before that she'd take care of Cooper when he got up this morning.

It had been a long night. On the drive back to town, she had told Dusty and Dillon everything that had transpired between her and Greg. She'd wept and railed as she'd recounted the time from when Greg had grabbed her at the café to when they'd rescued her. Through it all Dusty's arm had been around her, silently supporting, quietly loving.

Once back in town, she'd insisted Dillon drive her directly to Juanita's home. She needed her son.

She'd needed to feel his little body snuggled with hers. She'd wanted to kiss him a million times to assure herself that they were really both okay.

They'd brought Cooper back to Cassie's place, where Trisha had tucked the happy little boy into bed.

After that Dillon had continued to question her until the wee hours of the morning. When finally he'd left Cassie's house, Dusty had gone to his bunkhouse and Trisha had crashed into bed. She'd slept hard and deep without any nightmares to plague her.

She rolled over on her side to face the sun and smiled. The danger was gone and she could fully embrace her future with Dusty. They would find a place to live and eventually get married and hopefully give Cooper a brother or a sister.

Her heart swelled with the vision of real happiness. In that cabin with Greg, she'd been so afraid that she had no future at all, and now the future stretched out before her with a tantalizing sweet promise.

Suddenly she didn't want to stay in bed to waste another minute. It took her only minutes to shower and dress in a pair of shorts and a T-shirt and head down the stairs.

Cooper and Cassie were in the kitchen at the table. Cooper was coloring a picture and Cassie had a cup of coffee in front of her.

"Mommy!" Cooper jumped down from the chair and greeted her with a hug around her waist. "Cassie said I should be quiet this morning 'cause you had a long night." He leaned away from her and looked up. "Did you have a long night?"

"I did." She picked him up and carried him back to his chair. "But now the sun is shining and I'm here with you and everything is wonderful."

"Get a cup of coffee, it only makes everything more wonderful," Cassie said. Trisha laughed and got a cup and then joined them at the table.

"I'm coloring a picture for Dusty," Cooper said. "You were lost, but I knowed he would find you. Look, it's a picture of Jupiner."

Trisha laughed again, not sure whether to correct his grammar or the name of Dusty's horse. "Has Dusty been by this morning?"

"Not yet," Cassie replied.

For the next half an hour Cassie and Trisha drank coffee and chatted with Cooper. When he finished with his picture, Cassie found a magnet and hung it on the front of the refrigerator.

"Now when Dusty comes by you'll know right where it is and you can give it to him," she said to Cooper. "He'll be so happy to see it."

But lunchtime came and went without Dusty coming to the house. Trisha wasn't so concerned by his lack of an appearance. After all, it had been a late night for him, too, and he had daily chores to get through.

It wasn't until dinner was over that she began to worry why she hadn't seen him or heard from him throughout the day. She called his cell phone several times but it immediately went to his voice mail. He hadn't returned any of her messages.

Anxiety built inside her as the evening hours

waned and she still heard no word from him. It was eight thirty when she gave Cooper his bath and then tucked him into bed.

Once Cooper had fallen asleep, Trisha went back down the stairs. Dark thoughts began to play in her head. Had her kidnapping made Dusty's feelings about her change? Had he decided that he didn't want a future with her after all?

Surely she was jumping to crazy conclusions. There had to be another explanation for his absence. But what? He'd sported the shadows of a black eye when they'd parted in the early morning hours. Had he suffered other injuries that he hadn't mentioned to anyone?

A new apprehension worried through her as she wondered about his well-being. She was pacing the great room when Cassie entered and sat on the sofa.

"Go talk to him," Cassie said. "I just spoke to Adam and he told me that Dusty is in his room."

"For some reason he doesn't seem to want to talk to me," Trisha replied. "I've called him several times and he isn't answering."

"Don't you want to know what's going on with him? I mean, it's obvious that something is off, right?" Cassie held her gaze. "Maybe he just needs some kind of reassurance from you."

"Reassurance about what? Nothing has changed as far as my feelings for him."

"Maybe he figures now that the danger to you has passed, you don't need him anymore." Cassie shrugged and smiled ruefully. "Who knows how men think?"

Trisha rolled Cassie's words around in her head. Was that it? Did he really believe that she'd only loved him because she'd needed him to protect her?

Was he so insecure in her love for him that he really believed she didn't want him now, that she no longer believed in the dreams they'd shared for their future together?

"Go on, Trisha. There's a flashlight under the kitchen sink. Use it and go down to the bunkhouse and talk to him," Cassie said.

"Cooper…"

"Will be just fine here with me," Cassie assured her.

Trisha flashed a grateful smile and then hurried into the kitchen. With the high-powered flashlight in hand, she went out the back door and headed for the bunkhouse in the distance.

She had no idea what might be going through Dusty's mind, but if he really believed that she didn't need him anymore then she was going to set him straight.

They'd just been to hell and back together. He was the man she wanted beside her for the rest of her life, the man she wanted to raise her son as his own. The nightmare was finally over and now was the time for them to celebrate and rejoice.

When she reached the bunkhouse, Tony was seated outside one of the rooms. "Hi, Trisha," he greeted her.

"I'm assuming you're down here to talk to Dusty." He pointed to the room next to his. "He's in there."

"Thanks, Tony," she replied. She knocked on the door.

"It's open." Dusty's voice drifted out.

She opened the door. Dusty was stretched out on the bed and sat up, his eyes wide with surprise at the sight of her. His right eye still bore the dark circle and a slight swelling of the blow Greg had delivered to him.

"Trisha, I wasn't expecting you. I thought you were one of the other guys," he said.

He raked a hand through his hair and his gaze didn't quite meet hers. She closed the door and leaned against it. "Why haven't you come up to the house to see me today?" she asked.

"I've been busy." Still he didn't look at her.

"Dusty, what's going on?" Her heart thundered a slow beat of dread.

He finally met her gaze. His eyes were dark and unfathomable. "What's going on is that I've enjoyed our time together, but after giving it all some deeper thought, I think it's time we said goodbye."

Her heart stopped. "Goodbye? What are you talking about?" She walked over and sat next to him on the bed.

"You're safe now. We know the bad guy wasn't Frank and hopefully you never have to worry about him. You and Cooper can move on with your lives. You need to find a good man, Trisha. Someplace out there is the man you really deserve."

She stared at him blankly. "Dusty, I don't want another man. I want you. I deserve you." She reached out and placed her hand on his forearm. He shocked her by jerking away. "Dusty, please help me to understand."

"There's nothing to understand," he said harshly. "You need to find somebody else to build a future with. I'm just not the man for you."

She searched his features. "Then you don't love me anymore? Everything you told me was nothing but lies?" Pain ripped through her. Had this been nothing more than his desire to get her into his bed? Had he just wanted to be the cowboy who finally got her to say yes to dating? No, she'd never believe that.

"Dusty, you look me in the eye and tell me that you don't love me," she demanded. Anger momentarily usurped the unbearable ache in her heart.

"I guess I'm not the man you thought I was. Now, if you don't mind, I'm tired." He stared at some point just over her head.

She got to her feet, waves of pain crashing through her. "I certainly don't want to be here if you don't want me here." She walked over to the door and opened it. "I don't know what's happened, but I'll never believe that you don't love me. I love you, Dusty Crawford, and nothing you can do or say is going to change that fact."

Tears burned hot, and before they could fall she left his room and slammed the door behind her. Thankfully, Tony had disappeared and there was nobody to hear the choking sob that escaped her.

Thoughts of Cooper and Dusty had been the only thing that had kept her strong during the agonizing hours she'd been with Greg. She'd clung to the belief that somehow they would all have a future together. It had given her hope when rationally she should have had none.

And now that hope had been ripped away and she didn't know why. She stumbled through the dark toward the house, tears blurring her vision.

What had happened between the time she'd been kidnapped and now? What could have possibly changed his mind? It didn't matter. The fact was that he'd told her he wasn't the man for her. He wanted her to find somebody else.

By the time she reached the house, she'd swiped away her tears, not wanting Cassie to see her a blubbering mess. But the need to cry still pressed tight in her chest.

"I take it things didn't go so well," Cassie said softly.

"He told me to go out and find a good man." She bit her bottom lip.

"Dusty is a good man," Cassie replied.

"You know that and I know that, but apparently he thinks I deserve better than him. I don't understand any of this. How could he just turn off his feelings for me?"

"Are you sure that he has?" Cassie asked.

Trisha raised a hand and rubbed the center of her forehead, where a headache was attempting to take hold. Still, the ache in her head couldn't begin to compete with the pain in her heart. "I don't know. I'm going to bed. I can't think anymore tonight."

"Good night, Trisha. Hopefully things will be better tomorrow."

Trisha nodded, but she didn't believe anything would ever be better again. She climbed the stairs slowly, her brain still working to try to make sense of what had happened.

He'd been so closed off, so utterly shut down. She grabbed her nightshirt in the bedroom and then went into the bathroom to change.

It was over. The promise that had shone from his eyes whenever he'd looked at her would never come true. The danger was gone and apparently so was Dusty's love.

She stared at her reflection in the mirror and lost the battle to contain her tears. She'd been so happy. She'd been so sure when Dusty had rescued her the night before that she was really going to get the happily-ever-after she'd yearned for.

She'd lost so much in her life. She'd truly hoped that the losses were finally behind her. She sluiced the tears away with handfuls of cold water.

Minutes later she got into the bed next to the one where Cooper slept soundly. It was time to leave this ranch. There was nothing to stop her from leaving now. She and Cooper could at least go back to the motel until she could find a more permanent place for them.

Should she just pack up and leave Bitterroot? How difficult was it going to be to remain here, where

Dusty would come into the café to eat, where she could run into him around town?

She squeezed her eyes tightly closed, wondering how everything had gone so terribly wrong. She fought against a new wave of tears and opened her eyes and stared up at the darkened ceiling.

A few minutes later she heard Cassie come up the stairs and the sound of her bedroom door closing. Trisha desperately wanted the oblivion of sleep, but she didn't get the luxury as her brain continued to race.

Maybe there was something wrong with her. In her short life two men had developed a sick obsession with her. Didn't that speak of something amiss with her?

No, she couldn't think that way. She'd take some responsibility for encouraging Frank, for staying with him far longer than she should have, but there was no way she'd blame herself for Greg. She wasn't responsible for his actions or feelings for her. Then, what had changed Dusty's mind?

He didn't say he doesn't love you. He didn't look you in the eyes and tell you he no longer cares. She drew in a deep breath and released it slowly on a shuddery sigh.

Is this the way you fight for what you want? Do you just give up so easily? Dusty's voice thundered in her head. He'd teased her about giving up without a fight. Was that what she had just done tonight?

She'd walked out of his room without any real answers. She was as confused now as she'd been when she'd gone down to the bunkhouse to talk to him.

She sat up. This was too important to give up on. They were too important to give up on. He'd teased her about fighting for what she wanted, and darn it, that was just what she intended to do right now.

Without hesitation she got out of bed and went down the hallway and softly knocked on Cassie's door. Cassie was in bed with her nightstand lamp on and a book in her hand.

"Would you mind listening for Cooper? I'm going back to the bunkhouse."

Cassie sat up. "You know I don't mind."

"I don't know what's going to happen, but I need some real answers from him and I'm not going to sleep until I get them."

"You go, girl," Cassie replied with a smile of encouragement.

Trisha nodded and then turned and headed down the stairs. She didn't bother to change out of her nightshirt. She didn't want to take any time that might make her hesitate or change her mind.

She grabbed the flashlight from under the sink and then went out of the back door. If Dusty thought she was just going to go away quietly, then he was sadly mistaken.

After all they had been through, after everything they had shared, she deserved something more from him than the vagueness she'd gotten earlier.

With each step, a rich anger began to build. He'd blindsided her. He'd rushed to her rescue and throughout the long night of questioning his eyes had shone with love and he'd held her hand in support. There had been no indication from him that his feelings had changed toward her.

If for some reason he'd decided he didn't love her anymore, if he'd reached the conclusion that he didn't want a life with her and Cooper, then she couldn't do anything about it. She'd have to go on and she would, but not before she understood what had happened to change his mind, what had made him act the way he had.

No lights filtered out from any of the windows in the bunkhouse. Her heart beat rapidly as she realized this was a moment that would define her future. She turned off her flashlight and set it on the ground and then knocked softly on Dusty's door. There was no reply.

"Dusty, it's me." She knocked a little harder.

"Trisha, go back to the house. It's late." His voice drifted through the door.

"I'm not leaving until we talk," she said and then knocked even louder. At this point she didn't care if she woke up every person on the property. She was not going away. She used her fist to bang on the door.

A light blinked on and then the door opened. "Jeez, woman, what are you doing?"

He stood in the doorway clad only in a pair of black boxers. His hair was tousled, but he didn't appear sleepy. She pushed past him and entered the small room.

She turned back to face him. "You've accused me in the past of not really fighting for what I want. Well, I want you, Dusty, and I'm here to fight for you."

He closed the door, ran a hand through his hair and stared at her with shuttered eyes. "We already talked. There's nothing more to say."

"I'm so mad at you right now I could spit," she replied.

He raised a brow and released a sigh. "Trisha, I'd much rather we part as friends."

"And tell me again why we are parting."

He leaned with his back against the door and looked past her as if something on the bare wall had caught his interest. "I already told you. You deserve a better man."

"I already have the best with you. Why would I want anyone else?" She studied him, wishing she could read the thoughts inside his brain. "Dusty… please, make me understand what you're doing."

His gaze locked with hers once again. His eyes were dark and filled with torment. "I didn't hear you." The words sounded as if they'd been squeezed out of the very depths of his soul.

She frowned and sank down on the bed. "What are you talking about?"

His muscles tensed. "You were in danger and you called to me and I didn't hear you, because I'm damaged goods. I'm not strong enough—I'm not good enough for anyone. Even my own parents knew I wasn't worth a damn."

"They were the ones who were damaged goods," Trisha exclaimed. "They were obviously broken and not fit to be parents."

He closed his eyes for a long moment and when he

gazed at her again they radiated a wealth of anguish. "I'm deaf, Trisha. I'm deaf in one ear and if I wasn't then I would have heard you when you called out to me and Greg never would have been able to kidnap you and take you to that cabin."

Deaf in one ear? Her mind whirled and she remembered the times when she'd noticed he watched her mouth, when she spoke too softly and he'd asked her to repeat herself.

She got up from the bed and moved to stand mere inches in front of him. "Dusty, I don't care if you're deaf in both ears and can't see out of one eye. You're brave and strong, but more important than anything is that I've seen the pure goodness of your heart, and more than anything I want that heart to be mine forever."

His eyes misted, but still he didn't reach for her. He didn't make any move, except she sensed his tension. She reached out and placed a hand on his lower cheek, where she could feel the faint stubble of whiskers and a tic in his knotted jaw.

"Dusty, it was a dark and stormy night and I had an arm around my throat when I yelled to you. A man with a thousand ears probably wouldn't have heard me. Let it go. What's important is that you were there when I needed you most."

He reached up and covered her hand with his, his gaze locked with hers intently. He seemed to gaze into her very soul and slowly the tension left his body.

"And here we are," he finally said softly.

She nodded and they dropped their hands to their

sides. "Dusty, if you let me go, then your parents win. If you push me out of your life, then Greg wins. If you don't take me into your arms right now and tell me that we're going to have the future together that we both deserve, then I'm going to scream, and trust me, you won't have any problems hearing me."

The shimmer in his eyes transformed into something different than impending tears. It became something hot…something utterly wonderful and momentarily took her breath away.

"I love you, Trisha. I want my future to be with you and Cooper. I want to be the man you both want and need in your lives." His voice was thick with emotion.

"You're already that man." Her heart swelled to fill her chest. "Now, for goodness' sake, kiss me, you crazy cowboy."

He grabbed her around the waist and pulled her to him. His lips captured hers in a kiss that held all of the promise of the future, all the love she could ever dream of for herself and her son.

Her heart filled with a joy she'd thought she'd never have. Dusty was her forever man, and they were going to live happily ever after with a little cowboy who believed he hung the moon.

Epilogue

"Is this going to be Cooper's room?" Cooper asked as he galloped on a pretend horse around the empty bedroom. He stopped riding in front of Dusty. "Dusty, is this gonna be our forever house?"

Dusty exchanged a glance with Trisha and then crouched down in front of Cooper. "It's got a great backyard for playing cowboys and a bedroom for you, one for your mommy and me, and another one if someday you get a little brother or sister. I think it looks pretty good, but the final decision is up to your mom."

He straightened up as Cooper ran to his mother standing in the doorway. "I think this house is good. When can we get a brother? Mommy, your final 'cision should be yes." He grabbed her hand and danced up and down.

Trisha laughed. "I'll tell you what, let's go look at the kitchen again and then we'll make a final decision."

"You two go ahead. I'll be there in just a minute," Dusty said.

As Trisha and Cooper left the room, Dusty moved to stand in front of the window. It had been a week since Trisha had come to his room and fought for what she wanted. The past seven days had been the happiest of Dusty's life, and he knew that this was only the beginning.

This was the fourth house they'd looked at to buy to start their future together, and he had a feeling that this was the one. It was located two short blocks from the café and had everything they needed to build a life and raise a family.

The negative voices in his head had finally been silenced, unable to be heard with the ringing of Trisha's love in his head, in his heart.

Trisha had also gotten a bit of good news. Detective Eric Kincaid from Chicago had contacted her to let her know that he was reopening both Courtney's and Trisha's mother's murder cases. He'd also told her that a tip had come in that indicated Frank was still in Chicago and had been hiding out with one of his relatives.

Dusty smiled. It wasn't complete closure, but it was definitely a move in the right direction.

There was so much to do. He had a feeling that Trisha loved this place and that this three-bedroom ranch house with its beautiful yard and country kitchen was going to be the forever home that she'd dreamed of. There would be furniture to buy and a wedding to plan and he wanted it all sooner rather than later.

He was smart enough; he was strong enough to be the man he'd wanted to become. He was a man who deserved Trisha's love, a man Cooper could admire and adore.

He turned away from the window, eager to rejoin the two people who meant more to him than anyone else in the world, the woman and the little boy who were going to be his forever family.

Dillon typed the last word on his final report on the Albertson case and then reared back in his chair and frowned. Because the cabin had been located in another town, in another county, it had taken a lot of coordination to get the paperwork ready for the DA in Oklahoma City who would be in charge of prosecuting the case.

Greg had been transferred out of the Bitterroot jail and to the lockup in Oklahoma City to await his trial. Dillon liked it best when his jail was empty.

Although, there was one person he'd love to get behind bars—the person responsible for the skeletal remains that had been found on the Holiday property.

He'd gotten confirmation from the lab that the skull Dusty had fished out of the pond was the missing one from the remains, but for the past several weeks he'd been unable to work the case because of Greg Albertson and his crimes.

Now that issue had been laid to rest and it was time

for him to focus once again on the decade-old crime that haunted his sleep.

With each day that passed, despite a lack of any real evidence, he was more and more convinced that the killer was one of the Holiday cowboys. All he had to do now was somehow identify which one of the men was responsible and then prove it.

* * * * *

MILLS & BOON®

INTRIGUE
Romantic Suspense

A SEDUCTIVE COMBINATION OF DANGER AND DESIRE

A sneak peek at next month's titles...

In stores from 10th March 2016:

- **Trouble with a Badge** – Delores Fossen *and*
  Deceptions – Cynthia Eden
- **Navy SEAL Captive** – Elle James *and* **Heavy Artillery Husband** – Debra Webb & Regan Black
- **Texan's Baby** – Barb Han *and*
  Full Force Fatherhood – Tyler Anne Snell

Romantic Suspense

- **Cavanaugh or Death** – Marie Ferrarella
- **Colton's Texas Stakeout** – C.J. Miller

Available at WHSmith, Tesco, Asda, Eason, Amazon and Apple

Just can't wait?
Buy our books online a month before they hit the shops!
visit www.millsandboon.co.uk

These books are also available in eBook format!

MILLS & BOON®

Helen Bianchin v Regency Collection!

MILLS & BOON®

Why not subscribe?
Never miss a title and save money too!

Here's what's available to you if you join the exclusive **Mills & Boon® Book Club** today:

✦ *Titles up to a month ahead of the shops*
✦ *Amazing discounts*
✦ *Free P&P*
✦ *Earn Bonus Book points that can be redeemed against other titles and gifts*
✦ *Choose from monthly or pre-paid plans*

Still want more?
Well, if you join today, we'll even give you
50% OFF your first parcel!

So visit **www.millsandboon.co.uk/subs**
to be a part of this exclusive Book Club!

SUBS_2015

MILLS & BOON®

Why shop at millsandboon.co.uk?

Each year, thousands of romance readers find their perfect read at millsandboon.co.uk. That's because we're passionate about bringing you the very best romantic fiction. Here are some of the advantages of shopping at www.millsandboon.co.uk:

* **Get new books first**—you'll be able to buy your favourite books one month before they hit the shops

* **Get exclusive discounts**—you'll also be able to buy our specially created monthly collections, with up to 50% off the RRP

* **Find your favourite authors**—latest news, interviews and new releases for all your favourite authors and series on our website, plus ideas for what to try next

* **Join in**—once you've bought your favourite books, don't forget to register with us to rate, review and join in the discussions

Visit **www.millsandboon.co.uk**
for all this and more today!